AD HOC

JUSTICE

Malania E. Reynolds

THREE SKILLET

Ad Hoc Justice

THREE SKILLET

www.ThreeSkilletPublishing.com

Cover typesetting and formatting by Farley Dunn

1855 California Map © by Farley Dunn/Used by Permission

This is a work of fiction based on actual historical places and events. The author has referenced certain historical figures for context and realism, but all characters are fictitious, and any resemblance to actual persons living or dead, except in a general historical context, is purely coincidental.

ISBN: 978-1-943189-46-5

Ad Hoc Justice
Legal Definition

ad hoc: 1: *immediate and of limited scope*

2: *concerned with a particular end or purpose*

justice: 1: *the impartial adjustment of conflicting claims*

2: *the quality of being just, impartial or fair*

Example: During the California Gold Rush, conflicting land claims required frequent *ad hoc* legal judgments to settle disputes among miners.

— 1 —

Susannah Clark loved to read. She had come upon that trait at a very young age when she hid behind her father's big chair and saw him standing at his desk in front of her, writing something on a piece of paper. She was intrigued and forgot that she was hiding from her brother Anthony, who loved to tease her.

"What you doing, Papa?" Susannah crawled out from behind the chair.

"Why, I'm writing a note, so I won't forget it later." If Ezekiel Clark was surprised to see his daughter behind his chair, he didn't show it. As the father of six children, he wasn't often surprised by their actions.

Susannah snuggled close to her father's arm. He was so tall and solid. She felt safe when her father was near her. "Show me what it says," she begged him.

He took her small finger and traced the squiggles of the words. "These are letters and the letters make words. The words express our thoughts and actions. There are many letters, and you must learn them yourself."

"Really, Papa, what is this letter?" She pointed out one that looked funny to her.

"That's a Q."

Oh, what a good letter, Susannah thought, and it sounded grand on her tongue. She went through the house, saying, "Q, Q, Q," all day until her mother and older sister Mary chastised her and said that was enough of that.

By the time Susannah was sixteen, she knew all the letters and could read Latin and Greek as well as American English. She had such a quick mind and sharp recall that her father let her attend lessons with her older brother, Anthony, and his tutor. Anthony teased and taunted her, but he didn't object because he knew that she was more able to grasp the concepts than he.

"Anthony," she said one sunny afternoon to her brother, "Why can't I attend your lessons with you?"

Anthony was a handsome boy, or so Susannah thought. She'd always respected him, even when he played pranks on her, once putting a pan of water beside her bed during the night so she'd step in it when she crawled out of bed. She had scrambled from the bed in a rush and was horrified. She'd wanted to prank him back but didn't think it should be in a proper lady's nature to do so.

"I don't know, maybe because you're a girl?" He carried a hatchet, and he chopped at small trees, felling them to the ground. It was a game for him, but one of the servants would salvage the small plants and chop them further for the kitchen fires. No one minded, as long as he kept his hatchet from the ornamental gardens.

"I'm smart; you know that, and so does Papa." She simpered, but only because she knew it worked. Anthony would plead her case, if she plied him with enough vigor.

"What's in it for me?" He held a thin sapling in one hand with the top bent over, and he stilled his hatchet. He straightened and looked at her appraisingly. His shoes were scuffed— as always—and his white cravat was sweat-stained from the sun. He'd unbuttoned his cuffs, and his sleeves were rolled to nearly his elbows. His forearms were sinewy and striped with fat veins. Small bits of bark from felled trees sprinkled them like ground black pepper.

"I could help you with your hard lessons." She smiled prettily.

"You could not. Do you know even one word of Chaucer?" He bent to continue with the tree.

"When April's gentle rains have pierced the drought of March right to the root, and bathes each sprout through every vein with liquid of such power, it brings forth the engendering of the flower," she began to quote, before he cut her off.

"Show-off!" He laughed, and with a firm strike, split the trunk from the root and tossed it aside. "You may come, if Father says. I'll hold you to your condition. My hard lessons may require hours of your time."

She ran to him and planted a kiss on his cheek, and with a squeal of joy, cried, "You must be the one to ask. I've a quick mind and sharp recall. You've seen that, but Papa won't believe me. If you ask, he's sure to give in. Please, Brother."

"You'll help me with my work? Without fail?"

"Without fail." She crossed her hand over her heart in one direction, then the next, forming a cross, an unbreakable promise from one sibling to another.

"Return this to the shed as a token of your sincerity." He handed her the hatchet. "I'm going to the pond to swim. Don't come near, as I can't get my clothing wet, or Mama will lash me with a switch." His eyes twinkled. He was already unbuttoning his shirt, as he looked towards the house to make sure no one was looking from the upstairs windows. "Thank you, Susannah, and I won't forget to ask Father."

She hummed on the way to the shed, turning the hatchet in her hand and inspecting the sharp blade. Her father had Harry, the gardener, sharpen the tool regularly, and now Anthony had put a nick in the metal. Well, she wouldn't tell, not so long as he followed through and shared his tutor with her.

The next week, she joined in the lessons with her brother and his tutor. Anthony teased and taunted her, from time to time, but he didn't object to her careful explanations of the tutor's lessons, especially as his understanding increased and their father began to remark on his steady progress. Susannah determined to be especially kind to her brother in every way possible, as long as she sat at his side, at the tutoring table.

But, Susannah soon learned her limitations, as she slipped into the schoolroom one day and sneaked the sword from the wall. She had seen her brother and his tutor practice their swordsmanship, and she wanted to be like her brother in every way. But, alas, she tripped over her skirts and fell to the floor. With tears in her eyes, she replaced the sword and crept to her bedroom, hoping no one had seen her foolishness.

*****

When Susannah was nineteen, she was introduced to society as her older sisters, Mary and Alisha, had been. She loved the theater, ballet and the opera. But, she liked best to sit in the parlor and drink tea with her mother's friends or read the books in her father's office.

"Little sister, always at your books, and never at the parties." Mary, now wife of Edward Dillingham, and her son, James, were home for a visit, taking over Susannah's room and banishing her to the small room at the end of the hall. She combed the boy's hair and primped at his silk collar. "How will you find a husband, if you never present yourself to the young men of the county?"

"I shall marry my books." Susannah didn't like balls, because she couldn't dance well. She'd been born with one leg two inches shorter than the other. The left foot was shriveled, and red puffy scars remained on her leg and ankle where doctors had tried to cure the affliction. Without her special shoes, she limped and stumbled her way across a room. She walked quite well with her thick-soled shoes, and her sister seemed to forget how badly she danced.

"Pshaw," Mary laughed. She said to James, as she buttoned his new linen jacket, "No one can marry a book. It's not allowed by Christian law."

"Dear sister would try." Alisha appeared at the door in a lacy frock, with a closed parasol in her hand, twirling it fancifully. "Mary, try to talk some sense into our sister's head. I wrote from Grandmama's with very good advice, but I think my letter has been lost among all the dusty law books in Papa's office."

"Sister!" Susannah was mortified her sister would accuse her of such a thing. "I read every word."

"Did you change your opinion?" Mary smiled pointedly as she flattened a rumpled pocket on her son's jacket.

11

"See, Mary? She can't deny she ignored my every word. Mama is taking me shopping for a new dress, but we'll return for supper." Alisha twirled her parasol and disappeared from the doorway.

Her sister Alisha loved to attend balls and soirees and the opera. She had been in Philadelphia for the season and had only arrived the day before, and for that Susannah was grateful. She had written a long letter telling Susannah she'd have to disown her, if she refused to be presented, but she was certain Mary would find success in seeing her through, and they could remain dear sisters. And besides, Mama would insist, and there was nothing to be done about that. Susannah had sighed as she read the letter, wishing her coming-out could be filled with the ballet and the opera instead. Better yet, if she could stand in a court-room, and address the judge and jury in an important admiralty case, she would impress them all with her skill and knowledge.

At least she would have her bedroom back. It might have been Mary's when she was unmarried, but it wasn't fair she had to give it back when her sister came home. It was hers, now, not a hotel room to be shared to people who no longer lived in the house.

And, so Susannah had endured the stress and tumult of her coming-out ball with fortitude and was glad when it was over. She was dressed in pure white satin, the bodice low and her shoulders covered with a pale pink shawl. Her hair was swept up in a knot on top, with two ringlets hanging low on her shoulder. Throughout the night's affair, she had smiled and waved her fan, as her sisters had taught her; but not once had she danced, to the chagrin of her mother. But, she was consoled to find that her daughter received three bouquets of flowers the next morning from hopeful suitors, and she declared the party

12

a success.

Although Susannah was gratified by the tokens of favor by the men, she was most impressed by the simple gardenia posy sent by her brother's friend, Simon Maxwell. She smelled the sweet fragrance and admired its velvety petals.

Mary and her son left for her home, and Susannah took back ownership of her bedroom and was content to find that her father had an important court case and asked her to assist him by searching in his law library for previous cases to prove his point.

— 2 —

On this particular morning in early September of 1850, Susannah was sitting high on a ladder reading a book in which she'd thought there was a court case settled twenty years before. A bribery case in the newspapers had intrigued her, and she was sure that if she were the defense attorney, she could help the poor hapless woman win her case. The door to the office opened, and in walked her sister Alisha and her suitor Philip Manning. They seemed to be arguing as usual.

"But, Alisha, you promised that you would attend the new opera with me, and now you say you would rather attend the Caruthers' ball with your sister and mother. I say, it isn't fair to change your mind, when you promised weeks ago." Philip had an angry frown on his face and his tone had become critical and demanding.

"I know I promised to go with you to the opera, Philip, but I didn't know at the time that Emily Caruthers' mother was having a ball on the same day. I cannot be at both places at the same time." Alisha pouted, and her face was red and flushed, having turned the color of the silk flowers sprouting on her layered skirts and across her plunging neckline. Her hair twisted around her head, forming a cotton candy halo and spotted with glittering clips to hold it in place. She flounced to the desk, pushed her wide skirts aside, and sat in her father's seat. She pursed her lips, her eyes downcast, letting a smile finally seep forth. "You'll have to ask someone else to go with you to the opera."

Susannah felt a sharp pain in her left ankle. She adjusted her position on the ladder, aware of the step pressing into her posterior, and she drew in a sharp breath when the wheel creaked. Neither of her victims paid it any mind except for Philip, who glanced at Alisha, then away, when he didn't see further explanations. He seemed ready to explode, and Susannah wanted to see what her sister would do. Perhaps Philip would ask her to the opera. She'd plead with Mama, telling her Alisha's beau couldn't be disappointed, and could she please go? She was filled with excitement just thinking about the costumes, the flickering stage lights, and the carriage ride home. Plus, there would be no dancing, and no one would be pointing out her malformed limb. She started out of her imagination when Philip began to plead once more.

"But, I don't want to go with another girl; I want you to go with me." He stood stiff and heavy before the desk. "I'll say it plain, even if you get your feelings hurt. I don't like this stubborn trait in you, although you're the most beautiful girl I've ever seen, with your blonde curls and big blue eyes."

Susannah caught him as he arched an eyebrow. Like that would work, and she stifled her giggle. He was a silly boy, if he thought Alisha would melt for that. Maybe he wasn't a good choice for attending the opera after all. He'd probably laugh when he should cry, or cry when he should laugh, and she'd have to laugh at him and disturb the other attendees. How horrifying that would be! Still, her face warmed at thinking of taking his hand and hushing him with her finger on his lips.

Alisha jumped from the seat, her roses flouncing, and circled the desk. "Well, I shall go to the Caruthers' ball. I'm sure if you attend, I might find a place on my dance card for you." She almost touched the silk sleeve of his coat, then turned her head, lifted her blonde curls in the air, and marched from the room. Through the door, her footsteps told of her progress on the stairs to the upper part of the house.

With a disgusted cant to his shoulders, Philip stared at the open door with one hand at his hip, his elbow jutting akimbo, and one leg forward, in a manner that suggested total bewilderment. He hit his hat against the side of his leg and walked to the large, arched window across one wall of the library. He adjusted the shutters to let in a measure of light and allow him to look outside, and he cursed, saying, "Botheration, woman! When you put it that way, I wouldn't darken the Caruthers' door if I held a special invitation in my hand. I shall ask Vanessa Palmer to the opera." He jerked erect as if that was the answer to his troubles, and he strode towards the door, saying, "Yes, I shall. That will make her jealous, and I'll win her over, yet."

As he walked out the door, his hat in hand, he collected his cane and disappeared. In the distance, the voice of the houseboy filtered in, wishing Mr. Manning a very good day; and the front door opened and closed, saving Susannah from the embarrassment of being discovered upon her perch.

She chuckled under her breath, pulled the book to her chest

and started to descend the ladder. Each step brought her closer to release, when she could run from the room and laugh gaily at her sister's silly foibles. Sunshine from the open shutter created an arrow of brightness across the carpet, and the library seemed to glow. The crystals in the chandelier picked up on the reflected light, scattering it across the space in small bits of color and textured shadows that made the room seem alive. Her thick shoe made every other step awkward, and placing her sole on the treads was done by feel, hidden underneath her wide skirts. She worked her hand around the fabric on one side, and she pulled it up to uncover the hated beast so that she could find secure footing. Holding the book with one hand, and her skirt with the other, made precarious going, but she was determined, and with precise steps, she was on the next-to-last tread, when the door flung itself fully open, banging into the brass umbrella stand, and sending three of the burdensome utensils onto the floor.

"Oh!" Susannah cried, startled. She took the final two steps rather abruptly, barely catching herself, and dropping the book she carried in the process. Panicked that her sister would see she had been atop the ladder the entire time, she looked for a place to hide. She saw nothing, except the davenport, and it was hardly an appropriate disguise for an eavesdropping girl to hide behind. Her brother, Anthony, and his friend Simon Maxwell, plunged through the doorway.

"Anthony, you frightened me!" She said the words with emphasis, as she knelt to retrieve her book. "I could have fallen and killed myself." She stepped away from the ladder, setting the book on a low table. Simon had chased her brother inside, clearly in some pretense of play—though she couldn't fathom what had them so excited—and he was very near where she stood. Philip had been dashing and elegant, but it was Simon she truly thought of as her second self. She wished him to notice her, but he never did, other than to tease her, as her brother once had. She kept just to where her skirt brushed the floor, hoping he hadn't caught a glimpse of her special shoe. It was never talked of in the family, and she didn't think he knew. She caught a whiff of his cologne and thought how nice he smelled, perhaps spice and soap.

"Susie!" Anthony came to an abrupt stop. His hair was mussed, and he looked at his friend and shrugged before turning back to her. "What are you doing in here?"

"I have the right," she began, already irritated. Then she looked at Simon and softened her voice. "I understand. I'm in a man's world, and you are men. I just need this one book—"

"No, don't explain, for you're always in Papa's office." He said it in a tone of exaggerated exasperation, and looked at his friend and shook his head.

"Just because I put my time to good use—"

He interrupted again, cutting her off, with, "Leave us, please. Simon and I have something very important to discuss."

"You won't quarrel, will you? Alisha and Philip were just having words—" This time she cut herself off with a hand to her lips and a secret smile.

Anthony looked at his friend and took a deep breath before pleading, "Now, Susie? Our conversation is very private."

"Alright; I'm leaving." Susannah gave Simon a beguiling smile and sent a loving glance toward Anthony. Retrieving the book she'd worked so hard to obtain, she walked with a little jaunt to the door and left the room. She held her precious book in her hand, already studying how she would defend those such cases as needed a woman's touch, if only she were allowed to do so.

*****

Simon had been friends with Anthony for all his school career. They had shared the same tutor in their formative years; old Father Grisham, a retired priest. Simon had tucked private notes in the tutor's books, hidden in such a way as to be secret, only to be retrieved by his friend far away. In this way, they had maintained their close friendship until they went to University, where they had met in person for the first time in the library, behind the dusty shelves of Shakespeare's prose. Since that day, summers and holidays had been spent in one another's company, and Simon had learned to admire the younger man's family.

Simon couldn't understand why his friend treated his sister in such a brusque manner. He didn't treat Alisha the same way. He doted on her, as a special treasure that might break or be bruised with rough treatment. Simon thought Alisha vain and selfish, and while beautiful, he wouldn't want to travel in a carriage with her, not for a long distance. Anthony also treated his older married sister Mary well, with respect, even. He deferred to anything she said, as if she were the voice of reason in every situation. It was actually tiring, and Simon was glad she'd long before married and moved from the house. It was only sweet Susannah to whom he was sharp and curt. Anthony had once laughed at him when he remarked on it, telling him he was an only child. What did he know of six siblings living in one household together? It wasn't all pies and cakes. And besides, didn't Susannah boss him around? He reminded Simon of the lessons she'd contrived to attend with his tutor. She deserved his curt attention, and he'd not let up no matter how Simon complained.

Today was Anthony's day to complain to Simon.

"Now, Simon," he began the minute the door was closed behind his sisters retreating steps. "I've told you before. This is a foolish move you're about to undertake. It'll be dangerous on the road to California—"

"But exciting!" Simon was having no part of this argument that had been mulled over, decided, and explained to his friend. "Come, now, my friend. You can't want to stay stuffed up in this big house with fancy shirts and bows on your shoes. Where's your sense of adventure? Come with me to see the world as it really is."

Simon dropped into an oversized leather chair, one with wings to hold in the heat of a winter's fire, although now it was turned into the room. The seat carried the impression of many a traveler's rest, and he changed his position for greater comfort. He adjusted his own flounced cuffs and pulled at a stand-up collar pulled tight by a thin cord of silk. His trousers, tight in the modern fashion, stretched taut across his knees, revealing a sturdiness that made his dream of crossing the country in a rude manner of transport more plausible than his well-coiffed hair might suggest. He motioned to the tall racks of books gracing one wall of the high-ceilinged room, and guffawed.

"What?" Anthony inquired. He stood at his father's desk and pretended to inspect an inkwell, when it was obvious he was biting his tongue at his friend's sharp rebuke. His gray jacket flared at his waist, with oversized brass buttons for decoration down the front. It didn't close, but revealed his vest of deep blue, with corded trim of soft yellow-infused saffron. A fob for attaching his timepiece hung from a pocket, but it was unused, as attested by the lack of any ticking from its internal spring. He looked up at Simon, ran a hand through hair that was going prematurely thin, and he crossed his arms as he leaned against the desktop.

"You cannot have me believe your father's dreams are your own. What do you want with a houseful of mewling children when there's a world of excitement out there, just waiting for us to toss off these fanciful clothes and tramp into the glorious wilderness?" Simon laughed at the prospect. He continually tried to paint the beauty of travel, of experience, of life to his friend, but it seemed he was too much his father's son.

Anthony looked away, as though hearing a noise through the door, and turned back to his friend. "You're now a trained lawyer. All your years of schooling, the studies, and the contacts you've made. Many people envy your opportunities. Papa will give you a good position with the law firm. And, I'll get to see you every day."

Anthony's eyes held something akin to pleading. Simon saw it and knew the cause. Theirs was an old argument, started when Simon first mentioned his plans to his friend. But, he was adamant. He was going to seek his fortune in the western United States. If he could convince Anthony to join him, the adventure would be so much grander, but if not, he'd go alone and leave Anthony to his glum and boring life. Even so, he loved his friend, and he leaned forward in his chair, and he motioned with one hand as he presented his case in the lawyerly fashion in which he'd been so expertly trained.

"Anthony, I've explained many times. My father paid for my education, and I've honored my commitment to him and finished at the university. I would be bored after a week in a stuffy law office among the lofty tomes and educated, pompous windbags who sit in judgment over the lesser mortals on this earth. I must have the freedom of blue skies and the open prairie, or I shall die an early death." He stood, and he posed as a courtly defender of a brilliant idea that others should grasp as their own. He lifted his chin as though presenting an astounding truth. "This life isn't about seeing the same people every day and walking the same streets as we walked yesterday, last week and last year. Without change, we have no life. The rules of the existing sovereign class must be broken if this country is to progress toward a brighter future! I see a challenge in the new state of California that I cannot resist."

"Yes, yes. I've heard your endless complaints." Anthony toyed with the umbrellas, saw those that had fallen, and knelt to retrieve them. He dropped them into the holder, and they resounded loudly. He took a deep breath and let it out, exasperated. "But, can't you see the law is about justice and order? If everyone were allowed to break the laws, there would be chaos and confusion?"

"Chaos and confusion? Who says anything about allowing everyone to break the law? I'll carry it all up here."

"You know what I mean. Be serious, Simon."

Simon held up his hand to stop the younger man. "Please, Anthony, my friend. My decision is made and I leave soon for New York. Don't ruin our friendship with your argument and stratagems to keep me here."

"Never!" Anthony looked appalled at the accusation. "I'll miss your company, that's all."

"Tell me, instead, about Emily Caruthers and her mother." Simon strode to his friend's side and clapped him on the shoulder. He knew how to shift this conversation from its dead end and back to a better track. "Must I wear my blue suit and silver vest to the ball? You know how I hate to dress like a peacock. I hear there are to be some dragoons at the ball. We shall have to step lively to deflect the girls from their fancy uniforms."

Anthony laughed, his good humor restored. Simon was pleased, and the two men left the library to discuss the charms of Miss Emily Caruthers and her flighty mother's ball.

— 3 —

Meg, the upstairs maid, appeared at the door, and she curtsied. Her hair was drawn back and tied with a black ribbon, and she had on a white pinafore with a black skirt. Her hair was damp, and she seemed out of breath.

"Meg, have you readied my ermine cape for this evening?" Susannah looked at her books longingly and wished she could find a way out of the upcoming events. Her mother was determined, however, and there wasn't much she could do about it, except fall on her bed in a fit. Even then, Mama would surely tighten her corset as she lay dying on the bedding and pack her into the carriage, regardless.

"No, miss, but I'm working on it."

"Where have you been?" There was still much to do.

"It's nothing, Miss Susannah. Your sister has needed my time."

"As I will, soon. What has she demanded of you?" She

loved her sister, but Meg's time wasn't Alisha's, alone. They were both going to the ball, and Alisha was much more capable than she.

"It's nothing." She curtsied, again, more a bob of her head than anything else.

"No, you must tell me." Susannah had read in her father's books that the proper attitude in a court of law was to be forceful. It was the way to get one's intention across.

Meg peered out the door to ensure no one was watching, and she took a step inside and whispered, "She felt her dress needed brushing. I told her I brushed it only last night, but she said it must be perfect. I hung it in her wardrobe."

The girls had matching gowns, but in different colors. Alisha had chosen a frock of pale green, telling their mother that it matched her eyes. It hadn't, but Susannah, like a good daughter, had said nothing and oohed over its bows and ruffles. She'd noticed—although she'd not really minded—that it was the same style as the one she'd selected. Now, Alisha had a dress of pale green, and Susannah's was identical, except in stark white.

"Did you brush mine, also?" Susannah opened one of her books and idly ruffled the pages.

"Of course, miss. It looks so pretty on the dress stand. I can bring it up at any time." She pulled a cloth from her waistband and dabbed at her forehead. "My apologies, miss. The water, it runs into my eyes."

"Never mind. Finish with my sister. She's having the hairdresser come at two, and you'll have two hours free."

"Is she doing your hair, also? I do so like your hair when its down. It's so pretty."

Susannah smiled indulgently and sent the girl on her way.

There was to be no primping into a magnificent crown of curls, ribbons and bows for her. She would have nothing but a wash and a brush. She would see to that.

By the hour of two, when Meg had returned with her white dress, Susannah was prepared. She'd been visited by the hairdresser, who'd seen her at one, who'd helped her braid her tresses, and formed them in her usual crown of braids on the top of her head. Her mother happened into the room, and at her instructions, the hairdresser worked in a few sparkling gems to give it additional shine.

"It's to mark the occasion," she said, leaning in to give her daughter a kiss on the cheek.

Then the hairdresser was off to fill Alisha's fanciful head-dress with a plethora of curls, ribbons and bows. Susannah was glad to see her gone, although she'd been friendly and helpful. It was the idea of the ball that distressed her. Balls could be fun, if she wasn't expected to dance constantly.

When the hour drew near, it soon became clear they wouldn't fit into one carriage. The ladies' skirts were far too bulky, and for a time confusion reigned. Who was to ride with whom? After much discussion and measuring of skirts, it was decided that two carriages should be sufficient, and the matter was completely settled.

Father and son rode in the first carriage, removing their top hats as they climbed aboard. Susannah didn't expect to see her father among the guests she'd mingle among. For many of the gentlemen, she was told, the entertainment was less about dancing than being seen in society. Her father liked to move among his peers as thoroughly as his wife enjoyed the entertainment, but he seldom danced. He had told Susannah that it was important to be seen outside the confines of the courthouse or his town office, and this was an opportunity he mustn't miss, for more business deals were made in the card room than on the dance floor.

In the second carriage, mother and daughters rode silently, spreading their wide skirts over the brown leather seats. "Mother," Alisha simpered, dropping her chin and pleading with her eyes. "May I ride on the far side, alone? My dress is so much prettier than Susannah's, and it can't get wrinkled before we arrive."

"She's right, Susannah," she replied, with a sharp look at her youngest daughter. "Alisha's dress must be perfect. If an eligible man should step forth tonight, your sister must be well represented."

"I don't mind, Mama." Susannah gathered her skirts to move. She attempted to adjust her position just as the carriage jerked, and she yelped in discomfort. She grabbed the leather strap to regain her balance.

"Botheration! I'll make the change." Mrs. Clark gathered her skirts and shifted her bulk to the opposite side of the coach. The long springs connecting the axles to the wheels squeaked with her movement, and the coach shifted from side to side, only settling once Mrs. Clark was firmly seated.

The coach's near horse had a moment of fright, as it turned the corner onto the long driveway leading to the portico of the Caruthers' home. A scream of alarm was heard by the bystanders. The animal had to be settled before they could continue. A groom standing just inside the portal came running with a cube of sugar, and within minutes the horse was calm and the driver was able to continue forward.

Upon their arrival, Mr. Clark stepped from his carriage first, nodding at the footman and pausing a moment for his son to

27

exit. He moved aside, tipping his hat to a few stragglers at the entrance. Anthony joined him, nodding to a few men of his acquaintance, as they waited for the other carriage to appear.

Alisha was the first out of the women's carriage, and she stepped lightly to the ground, calling, "How horrible that was!" It was apparent she didn't realize the true danger they'd been in. People were killed all the time with those big brutes, and truth be told, she was lucky there'd been several helpful people nearby.

Her mother withdrew more slowly, holding the footman's hand tightly, and pausing to gasp at every step. Alisha called to her, "Mother! You must tell Thaw to be more careful. Come, I can hear the music. We must hurry."

"Be generous, dear." She broke out a fan and pumped it several times to cool off before turning to ensure her younger daughter exited also. "Come, Susannah. No sense in dawdling. It doesn't suit a woman to be late to a ball. You want to have plenty of young men sign your dance card."

"Thank you, Mama. I'll hurry." She had intended to remain at the side during most of the events, safely out of the way. Her mother's words reminded her otherwise.

"My dear." Papa gave his wife a kiss on the hand, after the French style, and they started up the steps together. The receiving line was long, for over two hundred people had been invited. Each name was called out, and they bowed, curtsied or shook hands with Mr. Mathias Caruthers; Mrs. Caruthers, his wife; Mrs. Caruthers, his mother; and finally, Miss Emily Caruthers, the daughter of the house.

Once his name was announced, Mr. Clark soon departed; and as he walked off, he greeted his acquaintances and began to talk of politics or the law.

"Your father will withdraw to spend the greater portion of his time in a back room provided by the host," Mrs. Clark shared with her daughters. "We shan't see him again before the carriage ride home."

As soon as Emily Caruthers saw her friend Susannah approach, she rudely broke from the line in spite of the frown from her grandmother. She yanked Susannah's arm and pulled her behind a potted plant.

"He's here! I knew he would come if my mother sent him an invitation. Oh, he's so handsome. I must dance with him at least once."

"Who's here, my dear? Do I know him?" Susannah was used to Emily's enthusiasm, for her friend fell in and out of love every month. Susannah looked around the potted plant to see if a prince of the realm or a duke from England had arrived at the ball.

"He's Lieutenant Timothy Divine, a recent graduate of the Military Academy at West Point in New York. He's come to visit his parents before he marches off to some faraway military post to fight the wild Indians."

"Oh, I see. I forgot that Father said there would be dragoons at the ball. This Lieutenant Divine is here, you say?" Sometimes, Emily had a tedious habit of spreading gossip, of which Susannah didn't approve, but she was a good girl, if misguided. Susannah started walking from behind the potted plant, for she was sure it was not the thing for the daughter of the hostess to be seen skulking about like a spy. She saw several men in military uniforms about the room. There was one speaking to Simon Maxwell. Quite handsome, he was, but not as tall and impressive as Simon in her opinion.

"Oh!" An exclamation of wonder escaped Emily's lips. She

whispered to Susannah, "That's him, talking to your brother's friend, Simon Maxwell." Susannah gave the soldier a second, more detailed look. She wasn't impressed. She practically dragged Emily into the company of some friends.

"Virginia," she whispered to the first, a slight girl with her hair in trailing ringlets, something the poor girl's great-aunt insisted she wear. "What is that gown you have on?"

"Oh, this?" Virginia spoke with a lisp, but when she smiled, she was very pretty. She patted the generous cloth covering her bosom with one hand. The flower she wore attached to her wrist—a white lily—danced as she moved her arm, as if to imitate its mistress. The dress was a daring mix of last year's style resewn into something only Virginia could have worn, with a flamboyant bow at one shoulder, ribbons sewn along her skirts from the waist to the floor, and a flounce around her hem that disguised its extended length. "This is one of Mama's old frocks. Sincey—" whom everyone knew to be her old, colored housekeeper, "—is the best with a needle and thread. She transformed it to entirely new."

"I should have such good fortune." Emily fingered the banding on one sleeve longingly. "I want your Sincey for my own. It's not fair." She pushed her lips out in an appealing pout.

"*You* have a brand-new dress every year. You don't need a Sincey." Susannah wagged her finger at her friend, teasing her playfully.

"I suppose that is better." Emily giggled with a hand to her mouth. She stopped and pointed over Susannah's shoulder.

Susannah turned to find the lieutenant some few steps away, as if they'd drawn close to eavesdrop on the girls. She'd forgotten him in the conversation in which they were engaged.

"I say, Maxwell, there is a group of lively girls." The

lieutenant spoke as though the girls weren't present. "Do you think you might introduce me? I have only a short time in Boston, you know." The lieutenant pulled at Simon's coat sleeve and started walking toward them. Simon smiled, pretending he didn't see anyone but had no choice but to follow. He acted surprised to come upon Susannah, Emily, Alisha, and Virginia Simmons so quickly.

"Good evening, ladies. Allow me to introduce to you Lieutenant Timothy Divine, late of the Military Academy in New York. He's here visiting his parents. Sir, this is Miss Susannah Clark, her sister, Alisha Clark, Miss Virginia Simmons and the daughter of our hostess, Miss Emily Caruthers."

Having discharged his duty to his new acquaintance, Simon turned to Susannah. "Miss Clark, I hope I might have the honor of engaging you in a dance when the music starts." He bowed politely over her hand, while the other girls were twittering about the lieutenant, like sparrows on a bug.

"Now, Simon, you know that I don't dance." She fluttered her silk fan in front of her chest.

"Ah, but you must dance with me for I'm your brother's special friend, am I not?" They had had this conversation before at other balls and soirees in the years since they met. "I sense in you a natural shyness that keeps you from dancing, yet I must insist." He picked up the dance card dangling from her wrist and signed his name. "There. See my name, thus? I've engaged you for the slow waltz before supper. You must keep your commitments to your friends, you see." And, before Susannah could react, Simon bowed low before her and was gone.

She watched him as Simon walked to a group of men. She was shocked at his behavior.

"Can you believe that?" She whispered behind her fan to

her friend, Emily. "He signed my card, even when I said I don't dance. What do you think of that?"

Still, her heart pounded. She opened the small card, and there was his name, in his own hand. It was beautiful, even if she couldn't follow through. Just to dream of it was enough for the moment. Her reverie of dreams was shattered by Emily's smart response.

"I think he must like you very much. Let me see." She lifted the card, peered at the signature, and she giggled once more.

"That's so silly. Shame on you." She didn't say it harshly, though. Susannah imagined herself on the dance floor with Simon, her leg whole and well, and able to dance the whole night with him. They would step out, touch hands, and turn on the floor for a moment. It would be so thrilling. What she said to Emily was, "Even Anthony tells him I don't dance, and he shouldn't have pressured me like he did. I suspect he'll insist that I keep my date with him for the slow waltz. Maybe I'll be sick by then."

"Sick of being lonely and in love," Emily teased, grabbing Susannah's arm, and hardly able to hold her laughter back.

When the music started, Simon danced with Permilla Wilson, then with a dark-haired girl Susannah didn't know. She caught herself wondering what it would feel like to be held in his strong arms. Oh, botheration, she thought. He's my brother's friend. She moved to the chairs along the wall and sat beside her mother and an older lady of her acquaintance, Tamara Selwig. Her dress was very conservative, of dove-gray silk, with a tight bodice and broad, shimmering skirts. Fine, eyelet lace made a white band around the sleeves and along the neckline where it plunged into her bodice. Just under her skirts, sharply pointed black boots peered out.

"Ah, Susannah, will you dance tonight?" Tamara held a goblet of punch. She lifted it to her lips and took a sip. She smiled as she set it on a small commode at her side. The fine crystal of the glass clinked against the surface of the wood, light and clear, even against the music driving the dancers forward.

"I think not, although I suppose I'll have no choice." Susannah fingered her dance card, wishing either he could come and demand his dance, or leave so she no longer had to worry about it.

"Careful, my dear. That smacks of self-centeredness. You'll never get a man that way." Tamara smiled as she said it, however. "Look there. That's a handsome young man." She pointed to Lieutenant Divine who led Emily in a lively polka. The dance ended, and he took her sister Alisha's arm in a slower folk dance. Susannah found herself tapping her right foot to the music and blushed when Simon danced by with Virginia Simmons and winked at her.

"Oh," Susannah exclaimed. "I think I must move. My apologies, Mrs. Selwig. I hope you enjoy the music."

"You don't want to miss all the action." Tamara nodded at Susannah, encouraging her to take part in the dancing.

Susannah gave a small curtsy and looked for someone of her own age. She was beckoned by her friend Georgina Shaw, in a black and silver toile gown with flowers woven into her hair. She waited under a balcony on the far side of the room with several other friends. When Susannah drew close, she was greeted by Beth Latimer, her sister, Frederica, and several friends she'd seen in society. They spent several minutes discussing proper ball behavior, including the etiquette of assembling on the ballroom floor with the various suitors who'd signed their dance cards.

So engaged was Susannah in her conversation with Georgina Shaw that she looked up in surprise when a man stopped in front of her. It was Simon, and her heart leaped in fright.

"Good evening, ladies. I believe this is my dance, Miss Clark?" There was a gleam of challenge in his eyes as if daring her to refuse him in front of society's biggest gossips.

"Let me check my dance card." She slowly and deliberately lifted the card, hiding the fact that there was only one name inside. She was angry at his persistence, and she had no other way to make him pay. Running one finger down the card, she nodded as though she'd found his name, and she offered her hand as gracefully as she could in her embarrassment, and took the arm he held out to her.

"Mi'lady," Simon gave a short bow and led her onto the dance floor.

It was a short walk, but to Susannah, it seemed as though they traversed a dozen rooms. They navigated men in military uniforms, and others in coats and tails. One young woman wore a dress studded with pearls, and her gloves extended past her elbows. She hardly recognized the space in which they walked as the Caruthers' home, one where she'd played numerous times with her friend, Emily. Once she reached the dance floor, with the couples in line, each person poised to move his or her feet in the required patterns, and the musician ready to play, everything changed for her. Always before when asked to dance, Susannah had worried about tripping, or stepping on her partner's toes; but, tonight in Simon's arms, the music sprang into life, flowing throughout the room as a spring bouquet of flowers. Nothing could have been so beautiful. She moved her feet, and they floated across the floor as though it was a field of fairy dust. She felt light and gay. She imagined the tiny gems in

34

her hair sparkling in the light from the chandeliers and her face glowing with color. She wondered if she looked beautiful to the man who danced with her. As she turned and twirled, her white skirts billowed around her, and not once did she pause to register that someone might see her special shoe.

The music stopped, and Susannah was giddy with excitement. All around her, couples slowed to a stop, and light clapping flowed from the onlookers. She knew couples were speaking to one another as they walked from the dance floor, but she couldn't make out a word. The music still filled her ears.

"Susannah?" Simon prodded her with a smile. "It's time for the supper to start."

"What?" She gathered her thoughts and noticed the floor had almost emptied. "Thank you, Simon, but no."

He led her back to her mother's side without another word, except, "Thank you. I enjoyed that." Susannah watched him walk away, a question in her lovely blue eyes. He seemed to disappear from the ballroom, and Susannah could no longer find him. There was more punch and small slices of cake as well as tiny sandwiches, and lively conversation filled the nooks, crannies, and shadows of the great hall. The time passed like a summer shower, light, fresh, and quickly gone. The dance, the dance! It was all Susannah could think about, as she continued to imagine she might catch yet another glimpse of her dancing partner. Even though the Clark family stayed until two of the clock, Susannah did not dance again, although her sister Alisha danced many times, even with the lieutenant of the dragoons, much to the chagrin of Miss Emily Caruthers. During the carriage ride home, Susannah requested to sit in her seat alone, so that she could place a soft pillow under her special shoe. Her mother tutted over her, but Alisha had so many stories to tell that Mrs. Clark was soon distracted, and Susannah was left alone to remember her dance with Simon.

— 4 —

Simon felt pleased with himself as he made his way through the revelers who'd come to the Caruthers' ball.

"Simon, leaving?" It was Jerome Swaim, in his dragoon's uniform, with his brass buttons and flashing sword at his side. He'd met the man earlier, and they'd talked between them as they'd recovered their energies between dances.

"Yes. Walk with me, if you will. Have you kept the girls' cards filled?"

"Alas," Jerome bemoaned with a false frown. "Not as well as you. I noticed you with the youngest Clark daughter. I had been told she never dances. What a triumph!" They stepped by a large window open to the night, and Jerome pulled out a cigarillo and approached a lamp. He lifted the glass bulb and touched the smoke to it as he inhaled. The end glowed brightly, and he let out a great puff of smoke.

"With her sister, also." Down the hall, Ezekiel Clark had

37

noticed him and raised his hand, heading his way. He wondered what it was about.

"Only once, versus two dances? I bethink I know which you enjoyed more." Jerome smiled.

"The one is the greater payment, for I've worked harder to receive it. I think Mr. Clark is here to see me."

"I'll speak with you later." Jerome put his heels together, nodded his head, and turned and strolled back to the party. As he walked, he snuffed the remains of his smoke into the soil of a potted plant.

"My boy." Ezekiel Clark paused at Simon's elbow. The older man's cravat was awry, and Simon could smell the liquor on his breath. He waited as though expecting Simon to speak before explaining what he needed.

"Mr. Clark." He nodded politely.

"Follow me." Ezekiel crooked his finger and led Simon to a dark corner of the cloak room. "I should like to see you in my home office at ten of the clock tomorrow, if you please."

"Privately?" Simon asked the question, but the older gentleman had already stepped away. It was clearly a command, not a request. Had he committed some unforgivable social blunder tonight? Then it came to him. The older gentleman planned to offer him a position in his law firm.

It wasn't what he wanted. It was his friend's final attempt to keep him in Boston. His furrowed brow smoothed with the thought as he gathered his hat and cloak, and with greetings of farewell to several people he knew along the way, he stepped into the night, looked up to the stars overhead, and breathed in the cool air. He was going to California, even if Anthony thought otherwise.

He smiled. He had plans, and he didn't intend to let anything get in the way of his dreams.

— 5 —

At exactly ten of the clock, the morning after the Caruthers'
Ball, Simon Maxwell presented himself at the home office of
Ezekiel Clark. When his carriage arrived at the Clark residence,
he disembarked and asked the driver to return in an hour. He
took time to look up and down the street, as he listened to the
sound of the horse as it moved away on the paving stones. The
houses were tall, with tight patches of grass and clipped bushes.
It showed money and care, a great thing for a man who needed
to maintain his social position in the city.

He wore white trousers and black stockings and shoes, and
his shirt was a linen seersucker woven with light green thread.
His deep green velour coat was cut back at the waist, and it
extended to the back of his legs. A bright buckle graced the
front panel of his trousers. Matching buckles of a smaller size
aligned with his cuffs, giving his wrists a finished feel. His
chain for his timepiece hung limply from a small pocket, and

his upper pocket sported a neatly folded cloth. He had a simple cravat around his neck and tucked into the collar of his shirt. His top hat shimmered in the morning sun. His heart was racing and his hands damp with sweat, and he ran them several times the length of his trousers to dry them. He'd been thinking all night how he could politely turn down the position of lawyer in the man's firm, without offending the man, for he wanted very much to remain in the company of his friend Anthony and his sister Susannah.

He made his way up the steps and rang the house, using the lever aside the door. He heard the clamor of the bells inside the residence, and within moments, the door swung wide.

"Simon Maxwell to see Ezekiel Clark." He bowed the upper half of his body in a quick nod, and he held out his calling card for the man to take.

"Ah, Mr. Maxwell." Jimmie, the footman, pulled the door wider. The interior of the residence was still cool in the gathering heat. The windows were shuttered, except just enough to let in a small amount of light. This was a household yet to fully rouse from the previous evening's activities. "If you will follow me, Mr. Clark awaits you in his office."

Simon followed as Jimmie led him to the door of the office, and he scratched lightly on the panel. The scraping noise was answered with a deep roar to "Come in."

Simon felt like a frightened school boy as he stepped into the office and saw the gray-haired man seated behind the desk. The man's penetrating eyes gazed into his own dark brown ones, and he tried not to squirm or clear his throat of the obstruction in his windpipe. He waited for the man to offer him a chair, for he'd been trained well in the civilities due a man of Clark's reputation and character.

"Ah, Simon, do sit down, please. You don't mind if I call you by your name, do you? I find you around this house quite as often as my own sons appear to be." Ezekiel nodded at him, as he leaned back in his chair. A cigar burned in a carved, stone bowl, with the smoke winding lazily towards the ceiling. A glass to the side held a finger of amber fluid, whether it had been poured this day or the previous was unclear.

Simon moved to the chair closest to the desk. He didn't intend to let the minor insinuation bother him. His hands might be sweaty, but Anthony was his good friend, and he had never visited the Clarks without a fair invitation. When Ezekiel nodded and smiled, he knew he'd been tested for his character and other qualities, and the older man was pleased.

Ezekiel Clark adjusted his position in the stuffed chair as though ready for a casual conversation about the weather. He took his cigar and blew a few circles into the air.

"I understand that you're a few years older than my son, Anthony," Ezekiel started in a quiet questioning manner.

"Yes, sir, I'm four and twenty." Simon stopped, for in his classes for his lawyer's degree, he'd found that too much information was not appropriate in such situations as this one. He nodded his head as if that was all the man had asked for, and he was willing to give it.

"And, it's rumored that your maternal aunt is a member of the British royalty?"

Simon laughed, for that rumor had been circulated since the last war. "Yes, I believe she does have a far connection to the royal family, but, I fear the connection so remote as to be non-existent today. It makes her happy to think so, although she's turned against her relatives since they burned the American Capitol building in the last war. She's fiercely loyal to the country of her husband."

Ezekiel leaned forward and snuffed his cigar out in the dish. He sat quietly for a moment. "I've brought you here for another reason, but your honest answers convince me to pursue this one for a time. I also understand from my son's information that you plan to go to the western country, rather than join the law profession in which you've been trained." He seemed to have only a casual interest in the answer, but his hand twitched, as though this might be the deciding factor in a bigger game.

"Yes, sir. I desire to become an adventurer in California. I've spoken with my parents, and my father's agreed to the adventure. There is no impediment to the move, for he's made his nephew, my father's sister's son, Bertram McLeod, his heir in the case of my death, or if for some other reason, I don't return to Boston. It's my intention not to return, but to remain in the West. Perhaps it's my destiny to become a lawyer in California." And, Simon grinned, inviting the older man to join him in the jest.

"Aye, that might prove to be the case. A newly ratified state so far from our eastern shores is bound to be ripe for lawlessness. I'm sure good attorneys will be needed in the new state." Ezekiel cleared his throat and leaned forward in his chair.

Simon braced himself, for he knew the real purpose of his visit was about to be revealed.

"You're acquainted with my daughter, Susannah?" Ezekiel watched the younger man with an expressionless face, giving no clue as to the reasoning behind the question.

Simon was thrown off the track, and he knew that he must have blushed. He felt the heat rise in his face and neck. He opened his mouth to answer, closed it, and cleared his throat. "Yes, sir. You know that I've met your daughter, for I'm sure that you saw us dancing the slow waltz last evening."

"Aye, that I did. I also know that was the only time that she took to the floor. Dancing isn't her best achievement. Her best feature is her sharp mind. If she were a male, she might become one of the nation's brightest lawyers, or even become a United States Senator." He raised his hand when he saw Simon's eyes open wide, and he leaned forward as though to interrupt. "I see you're surprised that my daughter is as educated in the practice of law as you."

"I had no idea." He tried to think, remembering her in this very office from time to time, and remarks she'd made. "I suppose I knew she enjoyed reading, but yes, I'm surprised."

"That's why I've invited you here today. I'm concerned about my daughter's future. She doesn't concern herself with parties or social events like her sisters Mary and Alisha. She wants to hide herself in the library and read all day long. That isn't good for a young girl of nineteen. She should be out in the public eye. She's an excellent housekeeper also, and should have her own place in a family setting."

"I'm sure, sir, if you say so." The older man leaned even closer across the table toward Simon, and the young man found himself holding his breath.

"I've thought about how I might approach a man like yourself in the matter of an arranged marriage between yourself and my daughter."

Simon gasped but remained silent, waiting for the man to finish his thoughts.

"You're wealthy, so I cannot offer money. You have strong family ties, and a good reputation for honesty and integrity, so I cannot offer a better position than you might gain on your own merits and education. So, I've decided to try to gain your pity, your natural instinct for the weak and physically handicapped of society."

"But, sir, I don't understand your point." Pity? What was there to pity? Susannah was beautiful, smart, and from a good family. She was to be envied, only.

"No, very few people know the secret in our family. Susannah was the fourth child of my wife and very frail and sickly at birth. Her left leg is two inches shorter than her right leg. She has endured several painful surgeries to correct the problem, without success. She cannot walk without her special shoes, in which the heel of the one is raised to match the other. When she is without her shoes, she walks in an awkward, sideways, limping manner. Or, must often crawl on her knees like a babe, when the pain she suffers is intense. You can see how that would discourage many men from wanting an intimate relationship with her. She must have new shoes built every two years or so, as the older pair wears out. It takes the skill of an experienced cordwainer. I can see that may be a problem if you move to the western shores, but I feel that you are an industrious and inventive man and will find a way to overcome the problem of the shoes.

"The greater problem will be the inner, mental state, for she won't accept pity or charity, so has proclaimed that she'll never marry or have children. This would be a tremendous tragedy, for she would be an excellent wife for the right man and an outstanding mother for his children. I've watched you closely these last few weeks. You are the right man. You could share your knowledge of the law. You would benefit from her cooking, baking, and sewing skills, for she has been taught all the crafts of a female of the time, as have her sisters. You would find her a good helpmate, if you have the patience and fortitude to

44

accept the challenge." Ezekiel spread his hands on his desk, having laid out his case. "It's up to you whether you'll accept this challenge. Do you need time to settle this in your mind?"

"I should like to talk to your daughter, if you please, sir, before any decision is made." Time to settle this? He thought of Susannah and their dance from the previous evening. Of the other girls he'd danced with, and there were several, most had been empty-headed and giddy, and he'd been glad when the dance had ended. He'd danced twice with Alisha, Susannah's sister, and she was certainly comely, but she wasn't a girl to spend one's life with.

Ezekiel smiled. "I'd expected a flat refusal of my offer, and that you might be indiscreet with this news, but I see I needn't have worried. The man I've observed in the past weeks is the one that sits in my office with me."

"Thank you, sir, but I'm still confused." Simon saw the older gentleman start to frown, and he corrected his words. "I understand your proposal perfectly, but your reason for presenting it in such a manner; that confuses me. Why would I have refused so flatly?"

"As I've shared, knowledge of my daughter's frailty is closely held. That alone would have turned most men against her. Even so, I couldn't resolve in my mind not sharing this with you, for that would have been a deception of an unfair advantage." Ezekiel seemed satisfied with his explanation.

"I'm still unclear, sir. I've found your daughter to be appealing, and quick of wit, but wouldn't it be better to let our attraction grow stronger? Then it wouldn't matter, surely, at least not to me." Besides, Simon thought, he was leaving Boston. Marriage was the least of his interests at this time. He wished adventure, not the bonds of matrimony.

45

Ezekiel cleared his throat as though uncomfortable with his next words. "I noted my daughter's mannerisms and expressions as you danced last evening. She is evidently enamored of you, which is something I find alarming, as you have plans to leave the city. When I became aware of the closeness represented when you danced with her last evening, I decided I must speak with you, for I won't have her hurt." He frowned. "Think upon what I've said. If you cannot agree to this, I must ask you to leave my home and not return. I will not have her affections involved with a man who cannot return them."

Simon considered the situation for some moments, rising at one point to walk to the fireplace and place his hand on the mantle. He thought of the girls he'd known in the past, and he pictured Susannah holding a book in her hand. She was interested in learning, and that was a strong attraction for him. She was also charming and beautiful. He considered if her impairment was as severe as her father suggested, and he decided it didn't matter. If she would consent to marry him, he would extend the offer with all sincerity. He turned to Mr. Clark, walked to his chair, and standing, with one hand on the seat back, he nodded his head and indicated his agreement.

"You are most gracious, sir. How soon would you like me to speak with your daughter?" Simon knew his plans to go west had little flexibility. The journey was a long one, and he must time it properly, or he would fail, and he refused to do that.

"Today, Simon. It must be done before she becomes too involved to draw back her affections."

Simon looked Ezekiel in the eyes with a solemn gaze. "I agree to your terms, sir. I hold your daughter in the greatest of respect and will honor my vows to her when made." He smiled with relief at having the matter clear. "If she will have me; it must be her choice, without reservations."

"I agree. I ask only one thing. Let me present the proposition to Susannah as your own idea; that you've come to me with an offer of marriage. If she suspects that I've proffered the position, she'll refuse out of hand." The older man sat, a frown on his brow, and awaited the answer.

"She can be quite determined." Simon smiled. That was one thing very apparent from the years he'd spent at her brother's side. He agreed and waited as a servant was called to inform Miss Susannah Clark that she was wanted in her father's office.

Ezekiel pulled a tassel on the back wall, and Jimmie, the same footman who had let Simon in the door, appeared. He stepped just inside, pulling the door to after him, and said, "Yes, sir, Mr. Clark?"

"I need to see Susannah in here. Tell her not to dally, as we have business to discuss."

"Yes, sir, Mr. Clark. I'll inform Miss Clark right away that you wish to speak to her in your office." He grasped the doorknob, withdrew to the hall, and noiselessly closed the door after him.

— 6 —

After a late breakfast, Susannah reclined on her mother's Chesterfield, and being Sunday morning, she wore her pink toile morning dress, sewn with small flowers in yellow and red, and with only one petticoat to hinder her movements. It allowed her freedom even as it revealed her slender form. A wide belt of contrasting cloth cinched the waist. The sunlight from the window crossed the room, laying across her lap like a coverlet of brightest wool. She had her left foot balanced delicately on a small stool, and the other twisted up under her. Spread around her were needles and thread. She attempted to complete the embroidery her mother had encouraged her to start some months before, but each stitch seemed determined to prick her fingers anew.

She smiled as Alisha regaled her with tidbits of conversations overheard during her social escapades during the ball. In their conversation, they agreed that it had been much too crowded and stuffy, but the ladies' frocks had been colorful, and the gentlemen were polite and had danced well.

"Lennie Carver stepped on my foot. I was so appalled." Alisha had a separate embroidery project out, and she pulled a green thread through the fabric, tugging it tight. Her dress was of a lighter nature, in pinks and yellows, with fluffs and ribbons, and matching decorations in her hair. "I'm glad he didn't ask to sign my card a second time."

"Others surely danced well." Susannah sorted through her threads, needing a particular color of red. Unable to find it, she set her small panel aside and placed her hands in her lap, watching her sister. "I enjoyed dancing with Simon."

Alisha giggled. "I danced with him twice. I should think he found me quite beautiful. I think all handsome men dance well, at least the ones who danced with me."

This Susannah could not challenge, since she had only danced with one gentleman. A scratch came at the door. The girls looked up in surprise. "Come in," Susannah called.

"Miss Susannah," Jimmie the footman stepped in, and he gave a slight bow, "your father says you are wanted right away in his office, if you please."

"I? My father wants to see me? But, it's Sunday; I thought he would be at his club this morning."

"There's a man with him, Miss. They's been talking for a long time."

Susannah and Alisha looked at each other in puzzlement. Then, with her natural grace when wearing her shoes, Susie crossed the room and walked slowly down the stairs, following the footman. She scratched gently on the door and waited to be summoned inside.

"Jimmie, is that you?' Ezekiel called from the far side of the

49

door.

"It's me, Papa. Jimmie said you wished to see me." Susannah placed one hand on the door, and the other on the knob, with her ear close to hear his reply. The wood was cool to her touch, and she could smell the light odor of the varnish used to coat the surface.

"Yes, yes. Open the door."

She turned the knob, pressed on the wood, and let the door swing wide slowly. She crossed the threshold, slightly nervous, and looked to where she knew her father would be sitting, behind his desk. He returned her gaze with a solemn expression, and she quickly searched for the other man Jimmie had mentioned. It was Simon Maxwell, who had stood as she entered. Her heart started thumping so loudly, she was sure they could hear it.

"Come in, daughter, and sit down." Ezekiel indicated the chair opposite Simon, and she sank into it gracefully, her skirts billowing around her. Simon reseated himself as she did. "I believe you're acquainted with Mr. Simon Maxwell?"

It was a silly question, for her father knew they were acquainted. He'd been at the house many times with Anthony. She didn't reply, but instead gave her father a puzzled look.

"He has come to me with a proposal for your hand in marriage. I strongly urge you to accept his offer." And, after dropping that bombshell in her lap, Ezekiel stood and left the room with a satisfied expression on his face.

Left alone in the room with the one girl who had captured his admiration, Simon rose and fell on one knee at her feet. "Miss Clark, I've admired you from a distance for some time. Last night as I held you in my arms, my decision was made for me. I love you and would be greatly honored if you would become my wife and the mother of my children."

"You love me? But, how could this be so; you've never indicated a preference before today. I don't believe you. This is some joke that you and Anthony have dreamed up to mock me. Where is Anthony? I'll tell him that he's gone too far this time with his jests." Susannah was outraged that they would use her so. She'd admired the man, and he would do this to her? Tears began to form in her eyes.

"No, Susannah, my dear, this is no prank. Anthony doesn't know that I'm here. Please, may I sit beside you and explain my impetuous behavior? As you know, I will soon take the examination required for my occupation as an attorney, but I don't intend to practice the law here in Boston. I've made plans to go to California and take up land along the coastline, if I can acquire it, and perhaps start my practice there."

She nodded, her head lowered. She wiped a persistent tear from her cheek that insisted on falling despite her strong objection.

"Susannah, I'm telling you the truth. I came to your father today to ask for your hand in marriage. I know that my plans to go to California might not be the way to begin an advantageous life together. But, I must start making preparations soon. It will be a long, arduous journey, fraught with peril. The rivers may be flooded, or perhaps we'll encounter wild animals; maybe even Indian attacks. There will be depredations unheard of that you'll have to face as my partner and friend, but I'll try as best I can, on my honor as a gentleman, to protect you and love you all my life, whether short or long."

Susannah looked into the sincere face of the young man she'd only thought of as her brother's friend. She hadn't felt any particular jolt of awareness last night when they danced, as her friend Emily swore she felt when first she met the lieutenant of dragoons, other than that of enjoying the attentions of a handsome man. She had looked for him again, but only because she'd enjoyed the dance, not because she had felt anything else. Even now she couldn't find any emotion except surprise and dismay. There was no heart pounding or stars falling from the sky. She saw him as a nice young man for whom she felt nothing but kindness and friendship.

Susannah looked away, finding the window and the one shutter that was pulled aside. Outside a small tree quivered in the breeze, and she thought she heard a bird sing. Was this her chance, her only chance? She was a practical woman. She wanted marriage and children. She dreamed of a family and a home of her own. Would another offer come her way? Would there be other men who might find her attractive? She no longer wielded the youthful flame that drew men as butterflies to freshly bloomed flowers. She found his eyes, still watching her, the hope within still pleading. She pressed her lips together, clenched her jaw, and decided it was he she would put on trial. Let him see the evidence of what she was, and she would know the truth of his ardor and resolve.

She would test him to see his reaction to her disability. She would be the judge to his presentation of marriage on this Sunday morning. If he passed the test she might consider his proposal. Otherwise, she would cast him from her court in disgrace and shame.

Susannah raised her skirt to reveal her feet. She watched the reaction of the man seated beside her. His eyes immediately fell to her feet. He took in the sight of her shoes.

"Please, unbutton my left boot, and remove my stocking." Susannah knew that she was being immodest, but it was the only way to test his reaction to her disability.

"Are you . . . are you certain?" He looked to her eyes, puzzled. "If your father—"

"My father has left us alone, and he won't return until we've settled our business. If you won't do this, then there is no chance for me to accept your proposal. This is something you must know about me."

"If you insist." He knelt before her feet, and he took the unusual shoe in his hand. "The sight of your shoe doesn't shock me, but I do feel surprise that you make such a request."

"Because I should have higher moral values, not let a man kiss me on the cheek, much less perform an intimate thing like unbutton my shoe and lower my stockings?" She knew she sounded sour, but she didn't care. She was exposing her most intimate failing, and he would know a secret that had never been shared with outsiders. Once revealed, it could never be taken back. "I'm testing you, Mr. Maxwell. If you cannot prove yourself, you have failed my test."

One at a time, he unbuttoned the knobs of her shoe. He pulled it off her ankle and set it on the floor beside him. "Your stocking? If you'll undo it, I can remove that also." His voice quavered, and a sheen covered his forehead, as though nervousness was about to overcome him.

"You must see what I'm about to show you. Don't be alarmed." Brazenly, she gathered her skirts, worked her fingers underneath the cloth to unhook the ties to her girdle, and worked her stocking to just above her knee. "The rest is up to you."

As he rolled the stocking, he saw scars: red, angry, puckered scars on her thigh, her calf and especially the ankle. He held her foot gently in his hands. It was shriveled and deformed; only

53

the special shoe gave it a semblance of normality.

He looked up into her blue eyes, and said, "I'm so sorry, does it hurt often?"

"Only a little, when the weather is cold and damp." Susannah felt her anger and resolve melt away. Only someone who truly cared would have asked such a question. He hadn't drawn back in shock or dismay. She wondered if her father had told him about her disability. She had to know.

"Did my father tell you about me?" He ducked his head for a moment before looking up at her, and Susannah saw the truth in his eyes.

"Yes, he told me. It matters not to me; for I know you to be an intelligent and pleasant woman of high standards." A twitch affected the corner of one eye, telling of his nervousness. He smiled, however, and he didn't remove his hands from her leg.

"And, you want to marry me despite the leg?" Her heart beat wildly, wanting him to say yes, and hoping at the same time he'd refuse.

"Yes, I'll be highly honored if you will agree to be my wife."

Susannah wanted to believe him, but she couldn't trust her life and the future to him, without an outward sign of his honesty. She rose, lowered her skirts, and tried to walk across the room. Without her shoe, she stumbled, and a gasp of pain burst from her mouth. Steadying herself, she continued, as her left leg dragged and her right foot stepped out. Each time she lowered her left foot to the floor, she limped badly. Finally, she made it across the room, awkward, stumbling, and trembling with the pain. She was accustomed to her family seeing her in such a manner, but a stranger was too much. She crumbled into a mass of skirts, petticoats and humiliation.

Simon gave a gasp of alarm and ran to her side. "Please, let me help you."

"Go away. Please, go away. Call my father to help me." She burst into a loud cry of mixed pain and self-pity, as she lay on the floor of her father's study.

Simon took the girl in his arms and held her tightly. She wept fresh tears on his jacket, and he murmured soothing words of comfort. He took his handkerchief from his pocket and dried her eyes. "Don't weep, my darling. I love you, and will always protect you from harm, if I am able." He assisted her to the chair and gently helped her replace her stocking and shoe.

When they were seated modestly beside each other, he looked at their entwined hands. "I await your answer, Susannah." He held his breath.

"I cannot answer today, Simon. This affliction I bear . . ." She glanced away and her eyes filled once more. She paused as she blinked the tears away. After a moment, she turned to him. "Will you give me some time to think of your proposal?"

He nodded his head. "Yes, I will give you one week. I cannot wait longer, for I must soon start my preparations for the journey west." He rose and prepared to leave, then turned back. "Now I have two tests held before me. I hope I've passed yours. It may be that I will fail the second test, you know, and I shall never become an attorney; in such case my father will be most unhappy." He laughed. "Anthony will force me into a duel, and I shall be totally disgraced. Would you defend me against your brother?"

She looked up at him, her eyes still damp from her tears. She handed his handkerchief back to him, and laughed, her good humor restored. She observed him as he left the house in a pensive mood. She tried to imagine California. What would he do there? Wander, explore the mountain streams and the valley floors? She pictured wild animals, Indian villages, and Simon reduced to hunting and trapping. Providing for a crippled wife couldn't be what he had planned for his life.

She had a week to decide, and she already knew, a week wasn't nearly long enough.

— 7 —

Two days before she was to give Simon his answer, Susannah stood outside her father's library door. She caught a whiff of the varnish smell she was so used to. She placed her hand on the doorframe, moving it slightly to let the texture soak into her skin. Elsewhere in the house, Jimmie's voice murmured softly, and cooking pots made faint clanging noises. She had spent extra time on her hair and finally pulled it into a sober knot on top of her head with only three small ringlets curled behind her ear. She wore a dress of darkest blue, decorated with brass buttons in the front and one each at her cuffs. The neckline was tight around her neck, and dangling on a gold chain was the cameo that her mother had given her at her coming out party.

She scratched on the door and heard her father bid her enter. She turned the knob and swirled through the door, as though she hadn't a care, and saw her father sitting at his desk, writing something on a pad. He looked up at her entrance, and she shut the door softly and walked across the room, her skirts whispering on the multi-colored carpet. She gave a quick glance at the picture of horses that Ezekiel had bought only a year ago and had hung over his mantle. She saw the ladder that stood so the books on the upper shelves could be reached. It reminded her of the scene she had witnessed before the Caruthers' ball, of her sister Alisha and Philip Manning.

"Well, daughter, what is it? As you can see, my time is limited. I must have this brief finished before court tomorrow." He placed his pen on his blotter. A cigar curled lazily into the air, its smoke sweet and thick with odors. Her father's hair was askew on one side, as though he'd run his hand through it, not realizing it hadn't lain down properly as before.

Susannah crossed the room and stood, nervously shredding the handkerchief in her hands. "Father, I have come to tell you my decision. I have decided to marry Simon Maxwell."

He seemed delighted. He smiled and rose to come to her. "Daughter, this pleases me very much. I shall be sad to see you ride off on your bridal tour, possibly never to return, but I'm sure it's the right decision. He has a bright future ahead of him. I have spoken with one of his professors at the university, and he agrees with me."

"But, I must tell you what I've done. So, you won't blame Simon . . ." A tear escaped her eye and rolled down her cheek. She knew how her father could be, judgmental if she crossed him, but supportive if he felt she had a good case to lay out before him. It was important to tell him this before it came to his ears by another means.

"What's this? Tears?" Ezekiel waited patiently, and he patted her hand gently.

"I wanted to test him. You remember last year when Jason

Boyington asked for my hand, and then ran away when he was told of my disability?" She really didn't want an answer, and she was relieved when her father just patted her hand again. "Simon told me that he loved me and wanted to marry me, but I couldn't trust a man after Jason, so I told him to loosen my shoe and remove my stocking so I could test his reaction. And, oh, Papa, he was so kind. He didn't look at the foot with shock or anger, but asked me if it hurt. No one ever asks if it hurts, not even you."

She remembered her anger at Simon, and her brazen request. She'd been surprised when he'd accepted her demands so graciously. She'd been humiliated, despite her bravado, and rather than take the superior station, Simon had offered her something akin to love. It warmed her to think of it. She didn't love him, but she thought she could, perhaps, learn to love such a man.

Ezekiel removed his hands from Susie's and returned to his seat. "Do you feel you could love Simon? After all, if he accepts you as you are, that must mean something."

"Papa, I still didn't believe that he could love me as a woman wants to be loved, so I got up, walked across the floor, stumbled and fell on my face." Her face warmed at the admission, and she placed her hands to her cheeks. She sank gracefully onto a chair and leaned one elbow against the arm, grateful the cushioned fabric could give her support. The feelings of disgust at how she must have looked to him were a scratchy blanket wrapped tightly around her shoulders.

"Surely it wasn't that bad." Ezekiel chuckled as she dried her tears.

"Perhaps not." She could see the smile in his eyes and realized how she had dramatized the whole matter. Of course, she would stumble and fall, she had been so nervous of his company. "Thank you, Papa. Telling it puts it in a better perspective."

"That's my lawyer talking. If we take things in the proper perspective, it makes all the world of difference. My darling, Susie, I can see how it all happened, and how you needed proof of his love, and now he is waiting for an answer to his proposal? Am I to congratulate him and send a notice to the newspaper editor of your coming nuptials?" He lifted a sheet of paper from a tray on his desk, and he placed his hand on his pen, prepared do so immediately.

"Oh, not yet, Papa. I asked for a week to give him my decision, and now I'm not sure it's the right one; to go so far away from my life here in Boston; the opera and the art museums. This cross I bear will surely affect my husband's attention to me. Papa, what must I do?"

Susannah's heart was tugged two directions. She wanted the caring Simon seemed to offer, and she wanted to believe it might turn into love. She imagined Mary and her little family. She'd never thought she might be given the chance to follow in her sister's footsteps. For a moment, she imagined a little one of her own, dressing him in a cravat and leather shoes, or perhaps a daughter, with ringlets tied with pretty bows. Then her mind was swayed, and she could only imagine him tiring of her condition and casting her out in a pitiless and heartless manner. It was a fist on her heart, squeezing her until she thought she might explode.

"You must follow your heart, of course. But, also, daughter, you must see the practical side of the matter. You will undertake an arduous journey, at the end of which you have no way of knowing what awaits you in California. Are you willing to live the life of a servant, perhaps live in a hovel with no conveniences, and perhaps go for days or weeks without proper food and shelter? It will be your duty to tend the household chores and support your husband in his endeavors, no matter the cost to your personal desires. This must be paramount in your decision: the welfare of your husband, without regard to your own comfort."

"Yes, Papa. I'll marry Simon and be a loving helpmate. I'll go with him to the western country and bear the hardships of the wife of a farmer and explorer in the wilderness. Really, Papa, I think it'll be exciting. Do you not think so? Your wayward daughter will travel to see the great mountains and the wild Indians." She laughed again, her equilibrium restored and her humor aroused at her own jest. "Thank you, Papa, for your good advice."

She left her father standing in the room, and she crossed to the garden and opened the door, simply because she could no longer be inside. The air was heavy with impending rain, and in the distance, the sky churned dark and gray. She stepped to the stoop, and looking back at her family's home, took in a view she might never see again. She plucked a rose as she strolled the paths, thinking about the day. She wondered at her father's hand in the marriage proposal, but she didn't dwell on it. Simon had been kind, and she could see his integrity in all that he'd done. He had honor and pride. She was certain of it. If, together, they faced the wilderness and led many people to safety and peace, there could be no better life than that.

Susannah was satisfied. Jason had felt he'd be trapped with her affliction. Simon seemed drawn to her despite it. She'd felt an onus to agree to the situation whether she loved him or not. Now, she knew, no one was trapped, not Simon, not her, and not her father. The possibility of love made the difference. It wiped the stain from everyone's conscience.

— 8 —

"I'm here for my appointment with Dean Whitten." Simon handed his card to the footman. He wore a dark teal jacket, with his top hat and gray trousers. His boots were suede leather, soft to the touch, but with a stiff inner structure for city walking.

"Yes, Mr. Maxwell." Hagan, the footman, glanced at the card and back to Simon's face, giving him a smile. "If you'll wait right here." He opened the door wider, and he invited the visiting man inside.

Simon looked around the room. It wasn't his first visit to the Dean's residence, but it might very well be the last. Above the fireplace's high overmantle, a massive bison head dominated the hall. It was tatty in places, and Simon tried to remember the story. The Dean's father, no, grandfather had been an early explorer, and he'd taken down dozens of the beasts. This was the only one he'd had mounted, and it had come to the college when the Dean's wife could no longer tolerate it at their personal home. The opposite wall held two tall doors, the Dean's offices, Simon remembered. Both were closed. Hagan hadn't gone there, so Simon supposed the Dean was occupied elsewhere. The other two walls held the front door, from which he'd just entered, on which two massive commodes on either side held fringed oil lamps, and the wall directly in front of him, filled with a multi-paneled set of leaded glass doors leading into the residence's dining room. He fingered the small brush in his pocket. Looking through the doors at the highly-polished furniture, he saw no one and slipped the brush surreptitiously from his pocket, lifted each foot, and gave the surface of the boots a quick stroke or two, bringing up the nap of the leather. For all his expressed talk of his desire to go to California and leave the legal life behind, still felt apprehensive about whether or not he'd be successful at his examination for the state bar. His father had invested so much in his education, he couldn't let him down. He felt it necessary to make a good show for this meeting. He was here to set up his appointment for his law examination.

"My good boy, Mr. Maxwell." The Dean came striding through one of the office doors, surprising Simon. He held an arm out, with his hand extended. When Simon grasped it in greeting, he shook it once and released it.

"Good morning, sir." Simon nodded agreeably.

"You're right on time, and I appreciate promptness." He turned and moved toward the now-open door. "You're soon to leave us. Taking a position at Mr. Clark's firm? What a fortunate young man you are to have such an opportunity. You're here to set up your oral examination times, I believe." They were inside the office by then, and the Dean turned to him with a nod, waiting for his answer.

Simon held his top hat at his side, and he worked his dark, lambskin gloves from his hands. His attention was taken aback by an open door he'd always considered to be for storage. It revealed a long hall, down which he could hear the sounds of activity, that of a family with a young child. It made sense that the man's office would connect to the living quarters of the residence. Simon had known the Dean had a family. He'd just never thought of him as living with a family.

"Yes, I understand you have an opening, possibly tomorrow." It was a Thursday, leaving him the end of the week free. He hoped the man was able to come through.

"I believe that can be arranged. Can't wait to get to the grindstone? Mr. Clark must be anxious." The Dean pulled a sheet of paper from his desk as he spoke, and he penciled in Simon's name. "What, about one?"

"That will be fine. I must tell you, Dean Whitten, I don't think my friend's father expects me at his firm. I've made arrangements to travel to California."

"California?" The Dean seemed taken aback for a moment, then he smiled. "Ah, Mr. Clark is brilliant. Getting a jump on the competition. I assume they do have a court system in California?"

"I'm certain, Dean Whitten." Simon felt the tension ease, and he chuckled. "My first priority will be to set up living arrangements, perhaps with some land for growing things. The lawyering will necessarily come second, for a time."

"Very wise. There aren't many people there, yet. You don't want to get the firm going too soon. Make food your first priority." He looked down the new hallway, and he warmed as he smiled, calling out to a pretty woman in wide skirts with her hair wrapped in a colorful bonnet. She stepped into the room.

65

She had a broad, white collar that mimicked the bonnet's style. Similar cuffs at her sleeves completed the picture. "Hannah, have you met Mr. Maxwell? He's a forward-thinking young man who plans to start the first law firm of its kind in California. Can you believe? In California. Perhaps he'll find some gold when he's there. I hear everyone is."

"I'm glad to meet you, Mr. Maxwell. I hope your hunt for gold doesn't pull you from your duties as a lawyer." She turned to the Dean and spoke in a low tone. "Don't forget, Robert's waiting. Your game, Jeffrey. He's waited on you all week."

"Right, right. I'll be just a minute. Thank you, Hannah."

"Good luck to you, Mr. Maxwell. California is wonderful, I hear, and I'm sure you'll be very successful." She dipped her head his direction and disappeared down the hallway, closing the door after her.

"If that will be all, Mr. Maxwell, I'm sure you'll do very well on the examination. Tomorrow at one?"

"Rodger's Hall?" Simon wanted to be certain. He guessed he was more of a lawyer inside than he wanted to admit. Leave nothing unsaid that needed to be said, so that no stone was left unturned.

"I'm glad you asked." Dean Whitten leaned over his desk and jotted a location and handed the paper to Simon. "We had a little rot in the wall, and Rodger's Hall is getting a refresh. This is our new location. I'll see you there. Remember, no books, papers, or superfluous items. Just bring yourself."

"Thank you, Dean Whitten."

The Dean leaned out the door and called, "Hagan? Hagan, please see Mr. Maxwell out."

"Thank you, sir."

"Certainly. If you don't mind, my boy is waiting on me to

lose a game to him." He smiled.

Simon nodded and watched him open the door to his private life and disappear inside. He turned to see the footman beside him.

"Sir?" He stepped aside and waited until Simon passed, then moved ahead and let him out the door.

— 9 —

It was a very nervous Simon Maxwell who mounted the front steps of the building in which he was to take his oral examination that Thursday afternoon. He hardly noticed the blooming forsythia, the freshly trimmed lawn, or the smell of fresh paint from Rodger's Hall in the next lane. As he glanced over the building's façade, the mullioned windows glistened in the midday sun, seeming to be eyes accusing him of having forgotten all he'd learned at the feet of his esteemed mentors. His hands felt empty as he removed his hat and stepped inside. He placed it and his cane on the oversized, heavily carved hall tree that ran for a dozen feet down one wall. He was certain that all his weeks and years of study had disappeared from his memory, and he would be hopelessly lost in a maze of questions that he couldn't answer. He was pleased to see a man he knew well, a teacher from his second year who'd been a great help to him.

"Mr. Bower. How nice to see you today."

"You remember me." Bower smiled warmly. He was fully gray-headed. His midsection was as wide as he was tall, but he was a kindly man, not the sort one expected in a school filled with budding and ambitious lawyers. "I requested your examination, as I remember your sharp mind quite well. I wanted to be present when you surprised yourself with passing our little exam."

"Thank you, Mr. Bower." Simon wasn't encouraged. He was certain now he would embarrass both himself and Mr. Bower, who assuredly spoke more highly of him than was strictly accurate.

"Your punctuality is appreciated, Mr. Maxwell. If you'll step this way. Our little examination board awaits your presence."

Simon followed Mr. Bower inside, to see three men already seated, with books and sheaves of paper on small tables at their sides. His place was standing behind a slender lectern, with only a small, flat top on which to place a solitary glass of water. One already awaited him, for which he was glad, as his throat had gone dry as soon as he stepped into the room. But, it went surprisingly well. The names, dates and case details seemed to flow with smooth regularity from his brain to his lips. Information he thought long forgotten came instantly to mind when he heard the question to which it was referenced. At the end of the afternoon, he left the building, much more comfortably than he had entered it.

He met Anthony Clark at their club afterward, calling, "Anthony!" He tossed his hat into the air, uncaring where it landed, although it was caught handily by the footman who'd taken his cane. He was glad to see his friend again, and that they were once more on good terms.

"I can see a man whose schooling days have come to an end." Anthony strolled his direction, holding a pint of dark liquid, and with a cigarillo in one hand.

"In a few days, perhaps. I'm not to say what I was quizzed on, and you, my friend, haven't taken your examination, but I do know the cases we've studied. Make sure you know every one."

"Every one?" Anthony had his smoke in his mouth, and he yanked it out with a cough.

"Every one." Simon enjoyed teasing his friend. He stopped Javier, the elderly man who'd served as the club's porter since he'd first set foot inside, and he requested him to bring him one of what Anthony had. The dark-skinned man nodded, congratulated Simon on completing his examinations, and moved toward a bar in the back of the room.

For the rest of the evening, the two young men discussed the pros and cons of whether Simon might have passed the final oral examination. They were friends again, but there was a certain reserve in Simon's manner toward Anthony. They had become embroiled in a late-night discussion the previous week on whether Simon's dream to go west was a self-indulgent fantasy or practical reality, and accusations of pride and callus feelings were levied. It was better to stay on the neutral subject of the law, although Anthony still hadn't taken either his written examination or his orals, and any discussion on the subject, while a welcome respite from their earlier turmoil and Simon's continued preparations for his travels, must be broached with delicate care.

*****

When the new week started, to quiet his mind while waiting on his examination results, Simon stopped by his father's mercantile store.

"Simon!" His father was in his office deep within the building. The double doors were open, and he rose from his desk and strode confidently toward his son.

To the right, behind a soft goods counter, two men in natty suits busied themselves sorting items into cubicles lining the wall. One was on a low ladder, and the other handed him items as his hands were emptied. After a quick glance at their employer, they returned to their business at hand. Across the store, a female employee helped a patron. They looked through kitchen items, and the metal items clattered as they lifted and replaced them on a shelf. The ceiling overhead was covered with painted tin panels, installed to simulate the coffered and carved wood in the expensive homes of the day. Two large skylights filled the room with light.

"Father!" Simon said it enthusiastically, but he wasn't certain how his father would react to his last weeks in Boston. They had their plans worked out, but he knew his father felt a certain level of disappointment. After all, the chances of their meeting again once he left were slim.

"I have something for you to do," Jacob Maxwell threw an arm over his shoulder and began to talk to him in a low voice.

With his father's encouragement, he spent Monday and Tuesday in his father's mercantile store finishing several tasks that were assigned to him. He didn't contact the Clark family, assuming that Ezekiel would take care of the business end of his upcoming marriage ceremony—if Susannah accepted his marriage proposal—with his wife's help.

The results of the oral examination came a day later, as

expected, and Simon was qualified to practice law. It was a relief to his mind. His family gathered for a formal supper on the day he received his news.

"Simon, congratulations." His mother greeted him at the door before he could divest himself of his top hat or remove his coat.

"Thank you, Mama." He gave her a quick kiss on the cheek, then removed his hat and handed it and his cane to Williams, the butler.

"Have you changed your mind? Boston is a wonderful city, as you well know, and I dare say you'll find more pretty girls here than in that distant land."

"I may take a pretty girl with me." He grinned as he removed his gloves.

"So, she's said yes?" Her eyes held hope for his answer.

"She will. I think we're expected." He saw his father gathering in the dining room, and he led his mother by the elbow to join his aunt. He noticed she refused to even name his intended destination, and he smiled at her ability to put troublesome events aside rather than deal with them.

"Welcome, Simon. It's good to have you at home. It's like you were never gone." His father guffawed and let his hand sweep the room. "Take your old place, son."

"Thank you, Papa." He stepped behind his aunt, first, and helped her with her chair. His father waited, standing by his, and let Simon walk around to help seat his mother. Then, at the same time, they seated themselves and pulled their chairs to the table. Kelsey, the footman, brought them their first course, a clear consume, and their supper began. Oxtail soup came later, with lobster, fruit compote, and braised salmon. After a final course of candied plums, the presents appeared at the table, surprising Simon. He hadn't seen them arrive.

"For you, son, to impress your new clients in that far land. Make enough money to come home and see us again." His father gave him a gold pocket clock with a long chain. His voice broke as he handed him the device, and his eyes glistened with tears.

"You've always been my favorite nephew," his aunt said, as she reached and placed her hand over his.

"I'm your only nephew," Simon teased, turning his hand so that he could hold hers in his.

"So much more the reason for you to be my favorite. Here," she said, handing him a box wrapped in brown paper and tied with ribbon. He opened it to find the family Bible with his ancestors' names and dates back four generations in England, so he would be reminded of his background.

"Come give your mother a hug." His mother called to him, waving him over with her hands.

"Of course, Mama." Simon stood, and he pushed his chair in and leaned down to wrap his arms around her. She grabbed him tightly, gave a brief sob, and released him. She wrapped in his hand a very old ruby ring for his bride's finger. She told him, with tears in her eyes, to cherish the woman who would wear it, not the ring itself, for jewelry could be lost, but love lasted forever.

— 10 —

The day of Simon's answer to his offer of marriage didn't start out in an auspicious manner. The skies dripped, the roads were little more than puddles, and to look upward was to drown in one's own topcoat. The only answer was an umbrella, but the wind was too brisk to keep it open without damage to the spine.

Simon Maxwell, his topcoat dripping with rainwater, his hat pulled low over his ears, and his shoes uncomfortably wet, appeared at the Clark home, his heart tripping with anxiety, and yet, he felt a sense of excitement at the commitment he was about to make. He had spent the previous night in plans for the future, and he was prepared to present his proposal to his chosen bride on the scholarly basis that he was sure she would understand. If she rejected his suit, he would be reasonable and accept her decision in good grace and hope they would remain friends in the short time left to him. He sighed as he raised the knocker; the weather was not the good sign of hope that he would have wished, but then, life wasn't always as one wished it to be.

The knocker was answered by Jimmie, the footman, and he presented his card and asked to speak with Miss Susannah Clark on a personal matter.

"Mr. Maxwell, please come in. Let me take your wet things, and Miss Susannah will be with you shortly. You may wait in the front parlor." The man took his top coat and cane, but there was nothing to be done about his sodden shoes or the puddle they made in the floor. He was shown into the parlor. His eyes roamed around the familiar room, for he had visited many times as guest of his friend Anthony. The tall windows, instead of shutters as Mr. Clark's office revealed, were draped with heavy silk brocade, in bright florals, such as a woman would select. The walls revealed a patterned paper that coordinated in color, if not in pattern or style. A number of chairs were strewn about, several in the French style, and the Persian carpet on the floor was patterned with vivid yellow squares. He took a deep breath, reminded of what Susannah would be giving up to make her way to California with him. It wasn't fair, he was certain, but remaining to shrivel into an old man in an East Coast law office wasn't fair to him. One could live without Persian carpets. One was already dead without fresh air, open landscapes, and freedom to live one's life as one wished. He glanced longingly at a davenport but dared not sit, in case he should dampen the furniture with his clothing. He rubbed his face with his handkerchief to remove any excess moisture and was caught off guard when he heard a sound at the door. He hastily put his handkerchief back in his pocket and turned, his heart beating loudly in his ears.

Susannah walked with dignity and grace toward Simon. She

curtsied low and held out her hand; he took it and bowed deeply over it. "Good day, Simon. I have heard from my brother that you have passed the examination with high marks. This must please you, as it pleases me to know of your success."

She smiled, and Simon could see the teasing gleam in her eyes. He relaxed. This was going to be easier than he thought, for surely she hadn't come to reject his suit while teasing him in her regular manner.

"Yes, I have finished my course, and to tell the truth, am much relieved. My wish is that Anthony will have equal success when his time comes."

"Oh, la, he takes the low road, always grumbling about his studies, but he'll do well, I'm sure." She gave him a sly glance. "But, I believe you haven't come to talk of my brother. Please sit down, my friend." She sat gracefully in a heavy brocade chair near the fireplace and beckoned him to sit in the matching chair beside her.

He cautiously sat where she indicated, while hoping that his short stay wouldn't stain the covers. He gazed at the fire and waited.

"Simon, first I must apologize for my immodest behavior when last we met. You see, my friend, I had another suitor, and he was most unkind. When you presented your proposal, I was surprised and uneasy. I felt the need to test your reaction to my disability, before I could trust your sincerity. I should not have done so, because there was no reason for my suspicions. You have ever been the gentleman in my presence, and have given me no cause to doubt your integrity. Will you forgive my impetuous behavior?" She looked down at her hands in her lap.

"Yes, of course. I can understand your concern. It's of no consequence, and we shall forget it, shall we?"

"Thank you. Now, to the matter of your visit today. You must know that I have only thought of you as my brother's friend until recently. The thought of traveling to California gives me cause for doubts and anxiety, but also, I find the prospect exciting and challenging. I find that the thrill of adventure and expectancy of danger have taken my fancy, and I look forward to joining you in this trek across our American continent. I have full confidence in your ability to protect and defend me, if necessary. Sir, I'll be honored and grateful to become your wife and helpmate. I will be as Naomi in the Bible. 'Whither thou goeth, I will go, and where thou lodgeth I will lodge. Your God shall be my God, and your people shall be my people.' "

Simon felt excitement flood him. He rose and bowed low. "Thank you. I shall endeavor to be a good husband and provider. It'll be a difficult and harsh beginning, but we shall deal famously together, for I have a great respect and admiration for your intelligence and your beauty. May I kiss you to seal the bargain?"

"Yes." She stood calmly as he drew her into his arms.

Surprisingly, he felt an ardor at her touch that he'd not expected. He gazed at her in question, but she laughed, rose to her toes and kissed him on the mouth. Laughing, she left the room.

He stood dazed as Susannah disappeared through the doorway. He took a deep breath and sighed. Marriage to such a woman would be one of the most difficult challenges he'd undertaken. He didn't wait for the servant, but crossed to the entrance hall, retrieved his hat, cane and topcoat and wandered out into the rain, his senses whirling and the perfume of her hair lingering in his memory.

— 11 —

That evening, Simon Maxwell met with his friend at his club. The room, with its lacquered paneling and wainscoted walls, glowed under the light of numerous oil lamps. One or two windows, with their shutters still pushed aside, revealed the deepening colors of the building sunset. The glass in the panes seemed to glow with a life of their own. The air was thick and filled with the smoke of cigars and pipes, as the gentlemen of society retreated from the cares of home and occupation. It seemed each flickering flame was surrounded by a ghost of the fading day.

Squire Flynt sat in the overstuffed chair beside the fireplace, the tall, heavy, maroon-colored drapes hanging behind his head allowing enough of the fading sunlight through for reading. His afternoon newspaper covered his upper body, although the evening demanded it be banished to a garbage bin. Slashed across the upper portion of one page, it read, California Wins

Statehood, in large, bold letters. On the opposite page, shifting with the man's breathing, a bold title, although in smaller letters, proclaimed the discovery of gold in the western lands as the economic resource that would drive the new state's future. Occasionally the paper would shake as his hand came off the edge to clasp a glass of wine on the table beside him. His body was relaxed in his buff-colored pantaloons and feet enclosed in black-buckled shoes with two inch heels.

Near the opposite wall, not even pretending to read the book in his lap, sat Mark Wilson, Senior, watching the activity in the center of the room. His eyes had a curious look, as he squinted in the dimness of the room. The early evening shadows crept across the colorful Middle Eastern carpet, and he blinked in astonishment to see, as the large clock on the wall chimed the hour, that the day had grown so late.

Four men sat hunched over their card game in the White Hart Gentlemen's Club; sometimes quiet and earnest in their betting, sometimes loud and boisterous. The table was littered with liquor glasses, a still-smoking pipe on a glass dish, and chips carelessly scattered around the center. Colonel Raphael McKindrick, the most prominent of the four, dressed in somber black and a vest of the same hue, with a snow-white cravat now stained with drops of spilled wine, closed his eyes a second, and threw his cards on the table; whereupon, Nicodemus Delmar gave a shout of laughter and raked in the pile of chips, chortling over his win. A disgruntled Percival Vance, dressed in a bottle-green coat, his gray vest supporting his long gold pocket time-piece fob, growled his displeasure, but Magnus Prince, clothed in rusty-brown velvet from his high stiff collar to his brown leather, buckled shoes, broken only by the tan stockings covering his calves, said not a word, simply sat back in his chair and watched the other three players. He took a sip of his drink and called for another bottle.

The servant obeyed his command, left a fresh bottle of port at Prince's elbow and scurried back to the shadows near Wilson's chair. No one could recall later how the subject of the gold discovered in California came into the discussion.

"Rubbish! Gold, on the ground to simply pick up as one walks by? Next they'll be saying diamonds are the riches of Africa, and all African women will wear them like the queen of England." Delmar guffawed as he pawed through his new-found wealth.

"Nay, my friend." McKindrick corrected his companion with a sharp tone. His eyes followed Delmar's hands as he sorted through the funds, much of it from McKindrick's pocketbook. "The news from Sacramento comes well substantiated. There's gold, as certain as you've won that pile of funds."

"News? What news?" That was Prince. "Are you speaking of our new state? If so, the real question is whether California will be a free state or slave." He pointed to the newspaper covering Squire Flynt, as he held the port in his hand, and he tipped a portion into a glass. Most of it made it inside, and he returned the lighter bottle to the tabletop.

"We were speaking of the newfound gold lying atop the ground. Ships at anchor, the cargo abandoned by their crew and captain, some ten deep at the wharfs. If the ill-restrained men aren't corralled, soon there'll be no harbor to speak of. The city will extend clear to the ocean." McKindrick still watched Delmar's hands.

"I cannot imagine such," Delmar blustered. His laughter was gone, and his riches nearly were, as he continued to pack the coins and paper bills into his ever-bulging purse. His eyes had darkened, either from the opportunity missed or from the perceived rebuke from his peers.

"And yet it's so. Delmar, if you were half as smart as you think you are, you'd be a successful man." McKindrick snorted in derision. He finally looked away from Delmar's empty hands, and he called, "Abner, a cigarillo, please, and two fingers of whiskey."

"So, the rumors are true." Vance had picked up the cards, leaving the others to their business, and he shuffled them with dexterity. The hissing of the air as the cards snapped against each other was a static background to the noise of the men's discussion. "I shan't be surprised if half Boston is on the road to California by the time the sun tips over Saint Matthew's Church in the morning."

"No one said Boston was leaving on a foolhardy goose chase to collect gold from the California hills. Heavens, man, most of us here would hardly know California if it flew up our pantaloons and whistled at us." McKindrick rapped the table top in a right good humor.

Growing bored with the discussion, Delmar stood and mentioned that his daughter-in-law would be expecting him home for a late supper. He took the bottle and his still-smoking cigar and departed the club.

"Do you desire to find a fourth and make another play for it?" Vance still shuffled the cards.

"Man, I've about lost my shirt." McKindrick blew out his cheeks. He looked less perturbed than his words might suggest.

"Win a portion of it back." Vance shrugged, but he kept the cards in motion.

With Prince's encouragement, McKindrick gave in, called to Buggy McPhearson, a rail-thin man with short legs and a neck that made up for them, and they soon had a fourth. The men continued their game, with lively banter and much exchange of funds from hand to hand.

Anthony Clark, his eyes following Delmar as he left the room, took another sip of brandy and growled to the servant to bring another bottle.

"So, Simon. I can't convince you to stay." He took the fresh bottle and sloshed a bit into a tumbler. He looked at Simon with something akin to disappointment, and he threw the liquor back hard, letting it go down in a single slug.

"Are you afraid you're losing a sister?" Simon clapped him on the shoulder. He took the bottle, held it to the light to read the label and smiled. He poured some into his glass and turned to Anthony to see him looking hard at him.

"I'm afraid I'm losing a friend. That's my liquor. Be grateful. It might be the last time you drink at my expense." He nodded at the partially filled glass in Simon's hand.

"So it is." He lifted it and took it down. When through, he leaned on the counter, resting his elbows, and looked at his friend. "See it the way I do. You're gaining a brother-in-law. We'll be true brothers, now."

"It won't be the same with you on the far side of the country."

Across the room, Squire Flynt laid aside his newspaper and rose to take his leave. He sauntered by the card table, where he caused a welcome respite, with a pithy comment. "Boys, anyone getting rich tonight?"

"The rich one's already gone." Prince blew out the words but kept his eyes on his cards. McPhearson laid one down, and Prince's eyes followed it, a quick smile forming in his lips before disappearing again.

"What's his hand look like, Squire?" McKindrick rapped the table, looking up at Flynt with a grin. "Got five aces in that hand, does he?"

That set the men laughing, and Flynt gave the men a last salute and a casual wave of the hand. He left for the door, tipping the servant generously as he passed by. The trio and their extra guest at the card table turned, glanced around the room and saw that it was almost empty. Wilson called, "More lighting. I could use a lamp at my side. And those blasted drapes, what's it take to get them closed?"

"Are you cold, Wilson?" Vance called to the man, giving him an amused look. "Or do you like complaining of the cold air?"

"Ahh . . . er, the night breeze always gives me the chills."

The servant put his hand to the drapes and drew them closed, and with a bow, placed an additional lamp by the man's side and lighted it from a slender candle. Wilson seemed satisfied.

"Heh, the hour." McKendrick pulled his fob from his pocket and clicked open his timepiece. "It's getting late, my friends."

"And the game is grown stale." Vance had few coins at his side of the table, and he rifled them with three fingers, sorting them as he did so.

"And unrewarding with Delmar gone," McKendrick mumbled.

"It would be. He has all your cash." Prince laughed. "I agree, however. My bedtime will be upon me soon, and the sun waits for no man."

"Then I wish my hat and cane." Wilson stood, and shrugging a top coat over his shoulders, made his way to the door; he gave a nod of the head to the servant, but no tip, and left the three men behind to finish their drinks.

"Until our next time." Percival Vance soon followed, yawning and staggering a bit as he waited for the footman to open the door. Before he stepped outside, he nodded to those left inside, and with a tip of his hat was gone. As the door closed behind him, the sound of a horse's hooves on the cobblestones outside came through, making a repetitive clopping sound, and a carriage's wheels clattered along after it. A voice could be heard yelling, "Whoa!" and the door was closed.

In the silence that followed, Anthony squinted at Simon, prepared to continue his tirade about the dangers of traveling to California, but hesitated as his friend held up his hand.

"Anthony, you know, I've heard your argument before; I shall not listen again. Besides, have you seen the paper?" Simon picked up Flynt's discarded newspaper and tapped the large letters across the top, and held it out to him.

"What do you mean?" Anthony glanced at it and back to his friend.

"Think of it, old man, an attorney in a new state! Before I leave to make my fortune, I must ask your assistance in my plans for the wedding. My father will demand that the ceremony be held in his own worship place, and I must discuss the dowry and the other legal matters with my attorney. It's old Marcus Selwyn, you know, long past retirement age, but Father clings to him, since they were at school together. I anticipate hours with the details of the settlements. You must support me in this; as I attend to the plans for the trip west."

"Yes, I can see that you'll be busy in the next weeks. Very well, I'll cease my admonitions and wish you and my sister a future of happiness and many children." He took a sip of his drink and laughed. "To think, that you have won the hand of my sister, Susannah. I thought her set on a life as clerk for my father and me. I'm quite pleased that you've chosen well. Now, we are truly brothers. I salute your good sense." He finished the drink and began to pour another when Simon stayed his hand.

"I think, my brother, that you've reached your limit. Come, I'll escort you home and wish you good night." He shook his head. "What will become of you, when you no longer have me to watch over you?" They both laughed as they called for their hats, canes, gloves and topcoats and left the building.

— 12 —

In the next few days, the activity around the Clark home increased ten-fold. There were preparations for two events to be taken care of: the marriage of Susannah May Clark and Simon James Maxwell and the preparations for said Susannah and Simon Maxwell, husband and wife, to travel to the city of New York to board a ship to Panama and the western coast. Items were suggested and discarded as not suitable. The seamstress and the cordwainer were called so that orders could be filled.

Trunks were packed and unpacked, then packed again. Boxes, trunks and burlap bags appeared with mysterious articles inside.

An equally chaotic atmosphere was developing in the Jacob Maxwell home, a few miles away. The Caruthers' ball was a fading memory, and the storm clouds had brought overcast weather and spitting rain. In the countryside, ruts were growing in the roadways like great serpents, ready to eat wagon wheels.

Small tree branches had broken free, and shimmering puddles infested every low-lying field with reflections of the muddy sky.

The city was only marginally better. Water ran alongside granite curbing, and the brick paving in the streets was slick with moisture. Water dripped from rooflines, and where there were gutters, they drenched unwary feet with disregard for class or rank. Even the doormats had given themselves up to toadstools growing in their corners. The carriages had their covers erected, and men hurried down the sidewalks underneath massive, black umbrellas, endeavoring to avoid yet another drenching for the day.

Simon stepped from his rented carriage, paid the carriage driver, and pulled his top hat lower over his face. The rain had lessened, but the wind was cold, and water still stung when it hit his bare skin. He shivered despite his overcoat, and he made his way up the walk to the front door. The butler opened it as he approached, and as he mounted the steps, bid him welcome.

"Staying dry today, are we, sir?"

"Not very, Williams." Simon leaned his umbrella against the rack on the hall tree, leaving it to shed its watery coating into the drip pan below. He slipped off his gloves and popped them against one hand before laying them on a marble-topped credenza. He removed his hat and shook it to disperse the excess water before handing it to Williams. The man helped him with his overcoat, draping it over his arm. Simon could hear his family in the back parlor, and he cringed inside at the announcement he would make. He pressed a palm to his temple to flatten his hair and turned when Williams cleared his throat.

"You look fine, sir. The family has gathered in the back room. Would you like me to escort you down?" Williams still held the wet coat, and he smiled cordially.

"Your hands are full, Williams. I know my way."

"As you wish, sir. Thank you." Williams turned, shaking out Simon's overcoat as he moved away.

Simon straightened his jacket. He brushed at the knap of his velour top, adjusted the chain on his pocket clock fob, and pressed the toes of his boots against the backs of his trouser legs. They came away dry and looked almost freshly polished. His father appeared at the tall doorway leading to the back of the house, and he greeted his son.

"Simon, son! I thought I heard Williams speaking to someone, and I was correct. Don't dawdle, now. We've had lunch, and we're waiting on the news. What information of a young man's life are we to receive, today?" Jacob Maxwell looked larger than life in a black coat, with a dark tie, and wearing striped trousers in gray and charcoal. White spatterdashes covered the tops of his shoes. The buttons down the side were dark, leather-covered bone, and they were neatly fastened., telling that he had been outside. His shoulders were dry, so his excursion through the weather wasn't recent.

"Yes, Papa." He had come to tell his family of his betrothal, and he hoped he appeared calm and serene. He approached his father, who clapped him on the shoulder, and indicated his son should lead the way.

"I see you survived the rain. Are you staying warm?"

"Mostly. The front hall is a bit cool." He'd thought it warm compared to outside, but once he'd removed his outer coat, he'd felt the bite of the broad space.

"The fire is quite warm in this part of the house. I'm certain we'll have you as warm as toast before you can give your aunt a hug."

They entered the room and saw his mother and aunt sitting together on a burgundy velvet davenport. Each end sported large, carved, marble-topped tables, with tall oil lamps with slender glass shades. Large potted ferns filled the corners, becoming a backdrop for overstuffed, brocade chairs in vivid birds and floral motifs. The high, paneled walls boasted numerous large oil portraits, and the richly carved ceiling was washed with a pale blue color. A piano-forte took up one corner, and behind it, a black oriental screen with ten panels reached twelve feet into the air. A fire whipped orange and red flames against a sooty firebrick backdrop, casting its warmth carelessly into the room. Wall sconces around the walls were filled with oil and merrily flickering away. The room felt warm and comforting against the oppressive weather just through the windows.

"Mama, Sarah, Simon has arrived. Come greet our boy before he slips away again." Jacob laughed, slapping Simon on the back, and he moved forward to take his place in a chair by the fire.

"Come, Nephew. Give your aunt a kiss." Sarah Fleming-Jones held her arms out, but she didn't stand.

"Good day, Aunt. You're looking well." Simon first kissed his mother on the cheek, then he leaned in toward his Aunt Sarah, allowing himself to be hugged by her, before he kissed her on the cheek.

"Simon, you said you had news." His mother spoke as she seated herself on the davenport, and patting the cushion at her side as she spoke. "I do hope it's good news."

"I think so, Mama." He glanced to his father, to see him watching intently, then back to his aunt, who had attached a small cigarette into a slim holder. The strange instrument was an affectation she'd picked up from her travels on the

Continent. She looked for the footman, and not finding him, held it towards Jacob, who dutifully stood, picked up an oil lamp, removed the glass globe, and held it for her to light.

"Thank you, Jacob. I should have waited . . ." She smiled wanly.

"I'm sure it did me no harm. Now, son, tell us the news." Jacob remained beside his wife, and he tucked his thumbs into his vest pockets, with his fingers spread out over his solid stomach.

"I've received an answer to my marriage proposal." He took a deep breath in preparation for the questions he knew would be asked. On one side of town were the Boston patriot society, those citizens being in Boston before the Revolution and descendants of English men of character and wealth. The Maxwells fit into this group, although Jacob Maxwell was himself a merchant. The other side of town consisted of Americans by birth and ancestry, for most of them didn't know when their families arrived in the country, or from which country they came. They included the merchants, clergy, lawyers, farmers and craftsmen who belonged to guilds in the city. This was the home of Ezekiel Clark, lawyer. In the America of the 19th century, such class lines didn't matter; all were American after the Revolutionary War.

"Do you hear, Sarah?" Simon's mother reached to pat his aunt on the arm. She turned to her husband, "Jacob, this is good news, isn't it?"

"What is their family name?" His aunt pulled on her cigarette, letting a long breath exhale through her nose, the smoke wafting around her face.

"Clark, Auntie." So far, Simon was pleased. The gathering seemed to be going smoothly.

"Clark." Sarah frowned in thought. "Ezekiel Clark, the law-yer?"

"I didn't know you knew them, Sarah," his mother said with a small laugh.

"Oh, yes, dear. Remember when Wilbur died and the estate was sold? Mr. Clark's firm handled the necessary arrange-ments, and quite well, too. In my day, a marriage between a Maxwell and a Clark wouldn't have occurred, especially in England where class distinction is practiced, as it should be," Sarah Fleming-Jones declared with a superior lift of her English chin.

"Now, Sarah," Jacob reminded her, "this is no longer the day of arranged marriages of old to further the peerage or the dictates of high society."

"Maybe so." Her chin dropped just a bit. "But, circum-stances being as they were, the marriage was accepted by both groups, and we were the better for it."

"Are you happy for me, Auntie?" Simon wanted to hear her say so. It would make a better start to his new life in California.

"She is, as are we all." His mother took his hand, and she kissed it. Then she looked to Sarah. "Isn't that right, Sarah, dear?"

"Which Clark daughter is it to be?" Sarah looked from one person to another, her eyes finally landing on Simon.

"Susannah. I'm sorry, Auntie. I thought you'd been told." Simon smiled warmly.

"Ah, Susannah, the quiet one. Not beautiful, like her older sisters, but she'll serve you well. I think you'll be very happy. You have my blessings, Nephew. You said you're going to Cal-ifornia. Do I remember that right? Sometimes I forget the most obvious things." She tapped her forehead with the hand holding the cigarette holder, then she placed it in her mouth and took a long draw.

As the evening concluded, Jacob Maxwell pulled his son aside into his office. He shared with his son that the first thing on his mind, after he accepted the fact that his only son had chosen a bride and was determined to remove to California, was to consider his son's education and occupation. He had graduated with honors from the University, and had taken his bar examination. He must now see that he had impeccable references to take to the officials in his chosen city of abode, and that he must do so before he left Boston. Next, he must settle all financial obligations. Jacob obtained the address for the Clark family and wrote a polite letter asking for a meeting between the families at their convenience. It was sent the next morning by special messenger.

— 13 —

A response came the following day from the town office of Ezekiel Clark setting a date and time when the two fathers could meet at his office. It was for two days hence, a Wednesday. The first meeting between Ezekiel Clark and Jacob Maxwell was stiff and polite.

"Come in, Mr. Maxwell." Ezekiel Clark rose from his desk as his clerk introduced his visitor.

"Thank you, Mr. Clark." Jacob Maxwell, while wealthy in his own right, wasn't certain just how to approach his upcoming relation. The man's social standing in the community was without fault, yet this was not a social call, but a legal one. Yet, if they were to be related by marriage, that added an unknown layer to the affair. He'd decided already to let the girl's father take the lead and see where the meeting took them.

They shook hands and bowed to each other. Ezekiel took the initiative.

"Let's start off on an amicable footing. There's no reason for our meeting not to go well. Since I am experienced in legal matters, let's first have a conversation on the matter of dowry and wills. Simon has mentioned that his nephew will be the heir if he doesn't return from the western country. Do I understand the situation correctly?"

"Yes," Jacob agreed. "The legalities have been attended to previously, but don't fear for your daughter. Simon has a personal income through an inheritance from his grandmother. Some would think him a wealthy man in his own right, and he's very capable of caring for a wife and future children." He suspected this was the real reason for the meeting, to ensure an income for the man's daughter if something should happen to Simon. He would be as concerned if he had a daughter, and he was glad this wouldn't be an issue between the families.

"Ah!" Ezekiel seemed to warm up. "Then let's move on to wills. I have one drawn up that might be amicable to you . . ."

The meeting continued until, with the more pressing financial matters attended to, each gave the other the name and address of his man of business, and all future negotiations would be settled between them. Next on the agenda, came the matter of a date and time for the wedding ceremony.

"My family has maintained membership in the St. Stephen's Anglican Church on Tremaine Street for three generations." Jacob nodded confidently. "Of course, your daughter will want to be married in the church of her fiancé's faith."

"I don't see how that will be possible. Father Geoffrey baptized Susannah, and she would be devastated to learn she wasn't allowed to marry with him in attendance. You understand, this is how it must be."

"I see. Shall we retire to discuss it with our clergymen in

private and find a resolution to our problem?" Jacob considered that his wife could perhaps call on the girl's mother. Perhaps she could sway her to influence her husband's mind.

"I find that acceptable, but the date mustn't be put off. If there's no agreement, I will insist on allowing my priest to perform the ceremony."

"Understood. Now to where the bride and groom will live after the wedding until their date of departure from Boston. I insist that the bride move in with my family. It would expedite matters regarding the preparations for traveling west."

"That's wisdom. It's a more convenient solution." Ezekiel nodded. He scratched notes on a sheet of paper as the discussion continued. "I'll see that her personal items are prepared for delivery to your home."

Minor additional problems and expectations were discussed, and the two men parted with a respect and a new regard for the other's position as parents of two westward-bound children.

— 14 —

In the days after the confirmation of passing his oral examination, Simon was twice given an opportunity to put his new skills into practice. The first time was two days after, when he returned to his rooming house one afternoon. It was a large and luxurious home converted for those of means who needed temporary housing in the city, complete with full services, including a footman and light meals. Chaucer Jenkins, a young gentleman just arrived in the city and new to the rooming house, was on his way out and stopped him on the steps to congratulate him.

"Ah, Mr. Maxwell. I hear you've received good news." Jenkins was in a top hat, though not of the latest style, and a waistcoat that seemed tight through the shoulders and too ample at the waist. His shoes were of good quality, but they needed a shine.

"Yes, quite." Simon nodded at the man. "Have we met,

sir?"

"Yes, once. I've just moved in, and you nodded at me in the corridor. I spoke to you and wished you a good morning, but you were in quite a hurry. Chaucer Jenkins." He thrust a hand forward.

"Yes, good man. I do recall, and thank you. How did you know?" He left the question unfinished. Good news about what, he wanted the man to answer. He was quite puzzled how this man he didn't know would have intimate details about his life.

"Quite by accident, I can assure you. I've struck up a friendship with Quentin Strasburg. He's in the last room on the top floor, and he mentioned you might be vacating, and your room was quite good. If I hadn't unboxed all my things, I might ask for yours. I told him I'm pleased with mine, and I asked if you'd be offended if I asked your reasons for vacating your room. He said you're getting married. Then I was quite pleased to see the notice in the paper while I was having my early morning chocolate. Congratulations."

"Thank you." Simon tipped his hat to him and made to walk inside. It seemed everyone knew, but that was quite acceptable.

"And you're now a lawyer, correct?" Jenkins removed his hat and ran a hand through his hair. It needed a trim.

"It's no secret. Just the other day I received the news I've passed my exams." Simon stood a little taller, both because of the new standing it gave him, as well as the knowledge his classes were done.

"May I query you about a concern I have about my mother? Not now, of course. I have a job interview, but later, if you'd find that acceptable."

Simon agreed, for eight that night, at his club. He acknowledged the man wasn't a member, but as long as he was with

Simon, there'd be no problem. It turned out that Jenkins was quite a nice fellow who'd come to the city to attend law school, but he needed to maintain a position to cover the expenses. His mother had a large home, but a mortgage had been taken on when his father was ill. If she could sell it, it would pay all his expenses and give her a small income, but the creditors were insisting the house be turned over to them, as the payments hadn't been made. She was afraid her equity would be lost, and she didn't know what to do.

Simon felt unaccountably pleased that the man felt he could trust him with such privileged information, and he quickly saw the way out of the situation. He relied on a class he'd taken on bankruptcies, and was able to quote the man several precedents that he thought would sway the creditors to postpone proceedings against his mother. He laughed at one point, telling him that he could use Simon's name as his lawyer. He was certain they wouldn't pursue his mother's property against the advice of a Commonwealth lawyer.

His next lawyerly advice was to his rooming house's footman, Franklin. The man was of late middle age, of good humor, and quite pleasant, if respectful. One evening, as the man was helping him dress to go out to a show with several of his university chums, Simon spoke to him about his upcoming wedding and the need to vacate his room afterward.

"My good fellow, I'll soon be married and leave this place for California. How can I repay your kind service while I've lived inside these walls?"

"That's very kind of you, sir. My employer—" and he caught his words, and amended his near-indiscretion. "It's nothing. I shouldn't have mentioned it. I appreciate your consideration, however." The man seemed quite pleased for Simon to have taken an interest in him.

"Ah, I see." Simon hadn't seen at all, and he thought about it the entire evening. He remembered how pleased Jenkins had been, and all for a few words that cost Simon nothing, and when he returned that night, as Franklin took his hat and coat, he propositioned him. "My good man, you seemed hesitant to speak freely earlier. Do you have a problem with your job, perhaps investments or legal matters pending? I'll gladly offer any advice I can."

"Sir, I'm not sure that would be proper—" He paused for a moment as if he wanted to say more, then he moved to place Simon's hat and coat in their proper place.

"Damn it, man, I'll say what's proper." Franklin was a good man, and Simon would do something. "I am a man of law, and I know what your employers can and cannot do if I give you advice."

"I . . . it's my age, sir. I'm being told I must vacate my job, that I must be able to lift and carry, and a younger man could do the job better. I have no other prospects, and I cannot afford to contest the claims against me."

"Have no fear, man." If this was lawyering, he'd gladly do it for free, at least for someone he knew and respected. "I'll write up a brief telling them I have found your services to be of excellent quality, and I would like to recommend others to rent rooms from them, but only as long as you are given a pension for your long service. I'll give you my father-in-law's card. How does that sound to you?"

Franklin smiled. "Thank you, sir. Your kindness warms my heart."

And so it was that Simon began to appreciate the education for which his father had paid so dearly, and how he might use his knowledge to help others obtain justice.

— 15 —

The twelfth day after passing the bar examination was Simon's wedding day. Franklin, the footman who serviced the rooming house where Simon lived, drew back the curtains and released the shutters to let the daylight flood in, calling to him in a cheerful voice.

"Good morning, sir. Today is your big day." The man, wearing a dark suit of durable wool, with a black tie, gray vest, and gray cotton gloves, turned his back to the window and stood, waiting for Simon to respond.

Simon slowly roused from his nightly endeavors of dreams and tumbled thoughts, and he pushed the covers aside. He swung his legs off his bed and leaned forward, his hands on his forehead, and his elbows on his knees. After a few moments, he looked up and gave the footman a bleary smile.

"Yes, Franklin, I suppose it is. Do you have my coffee?"

"Here, sir." Franklin stepped to a tall console beside the

door, and he poured from a silver carafe into a china cup. The black liquid steamed. He dispensed a small amount of milk into it and dropped in a single sugar before stirring it once and setting the spoon aside. He placed it on a saucer and turned.

Simon was already at the window. The sun painted him bright. His night clothing was of a subtle pattern, with thin stripes down the legs of his sleeping trousers, and a solid top with matching stripes on the lapel and the cuffs. The clothing was rumpled, bunched in wrinkled lumps from his night in the bed. His hair was awry, having taken a flight of fancy, and he would need a shave before starting the day. When Franklin brought the cup near, Simon took it gratefully and sipped a small portion.

"This is very good." Simon smiled. "Exceptional, I might say."

"Thank you, sir. Will you be wanting your shave, soon?" Franklin still stood to Simon's side, awaiting the return of the cup or any other help he might give his employer.

"In a few moments. Has the paper come?" Simon ran a hand through his hair, and he yawned, before shaking his head to wake himself.

"At your desk, sir."

"And my wedding suit? Has it been brought round?"

"In the hall just outside."

"I'm good for now, Franklin. If anyone else needs you, you may go. Check back in, though. I can't miss my wedding, or my new wife won't be my new wife." He chuckled, and he studied the gardens just outside the window, acknowledging the beauty of the coming day.

"Thank you, sir. The Scottish gentleman just down the hall has requested some of my time, and I must see the barber in to meet with Jenkins, the new man. I'll stop by afterwards to see how you're progressing with your morning."

"Thank you," Simon said absently. His mind was already on the wedding that afternoon. He had let Mr. Clark and his father jostle the details, and he'd not worried about it except for the small part he was to play. He'd heard his father was insistent Susannah and he were to be married in the Anglican faith, and that Ezekiel Clark was determined it would be an orthodox ceremony. However, it had been settled amicably, as Simon had trusted it would, and they would be in the church he'd been christened in, one that was familiar to him from his earliest days.

His least favorite time of the past week had been the two days of lessons on the responsibilities of family life and commitment. He had, at least, been able to spend a little time with his future wife, even if it was regularly in the company of her mother and the minister of the faith.

At three-of-the-clock, Simon was fully attired, in highly-shined, black boots, with trousers in dark gray linen, a silver vest, and a black cutaway waistcoat of raw silk. His neck was surrounded by a high cravat in white, the color which also rippled around his wrists from underneath his cuffs. His hair, tamed by pomade and a brush, was just visible underneath his sheared ermine top hat. His silk gloves matched his vest, giving him a finished look. Simon stood in front of a mirrored door, as Franklin attached decorative buttons and fobs.

"Am I finished, Franklin?" Simon eyed himself critically. His father was a famous and popular man. The marriage of his son was a major event no one wanted to miss. The church would be full of members and guests, and Simon needed to look his very best.

"No one could look any better, sir." He pulled a timepiece from his pocket and checked it. "The carriage will be arriving soon. We must get you to the west portico. If you will." He stepped away and opened the door.

Franklin, of course, remained behind, and Simon was left to make his way to the church, alone. He carried his cane with him, and tapping it on the back of the driver's seat, he called, "Slow, now. There's no need to be careless."

"Yes, sir," the driver called back, with a respectful nod of his head. He clicked his teeth at the horses, gave the reins a gentle flick, and with a jerk, they were off to the wedding.

— 16 —

Susannah stood in front of a looking glass, in disagreement with the hairdresser, Abigail.

"My dear, it's the latest style." The woman had her irons heated, and she'd described what she wanted. Curls, at least, or ringlets, if Susannah would let her. "It will be beautiful on you."

Susannah thought otherwise. Just because ringlets were popular didn't mean they suited her face. She had said as much, even to her mother, but in a kinder way. She'd felt awkward insisting, as she felt she should give in to her mother, but her reading in her father's books had given her a measure of trust in her right to make decisions that affected only her. She might be a woman, but even women had certain legal rights, if they wanted to fight for them. Even in her marriage, with its awkward proposal, she'd stood up to Simon and demanded to be heard. She would be heard in this, also.

"The latest styles might very well be beautiful *on some*

people, but I'm afraid I'm simply not one of them. Please pull it back severely, if you will."

Abigail sighed and made a last attempt. She pulled Susannah's hair back with both hands, began to braid it and pinned the whole on top of her head. With a comb, she worked a few tendrils free from around her face and, with great care, worked blue ribbons and white rose buds into her braid.

Once it was finished, Susannah had to admit she was swayed. "Thank you, Abigail, this is beautiful."

The effect was more attractive than she'd imagined. Her long white veil would shroud her face until it was lifted for the vows, so no one would see the hairdresser's handiwork until the vows were completed, but she could anticipate Simon removing the heavy veil to give her the kiss of confirmation after their vows were spoken.

When the clock chimed two, it was time to don her dress. It was elaborate, a thick, heavy fabric, lined with silk, and worked with pale blue ribbons. Teardrop pearls sprinkled the fabric, and a sheer taffeta layered it all. Her elbow-length gloves of softest kid and padded silk shoes completed the ensemble.

She gathered with her bridesmaids, including her sister, Alisha, and her good friends, Georgina, Beth, and Emily. They were dressed in a similar fashion, with their dresses mimicking Susannah's, but of course, not nearly so beautiful or elaborate. Georgina, Beth, and Emily held bouquets of flowers, but none so large as Alisha's. They included dyed blue roses, chrysanthemums, and a spray of tiny white Baby's Breath. The aroma was heady in the small church anteroom. The organ swelled in volume, and a lady-in-waiting opened the door and called, "They're ready, Miss Susannah."

"Thank you, Betsey." She smiled and nodded, before

looking at her friends, and they all giggled, even Alisha.

Mary, who was to be Susannah's matron-of-honor, scratched softly at the door. When invited in, she took the bride's hand and held it gently between two of hers.

"Susannah, my sister, I know we've had differences of opinion, and there were days you declared you didn't want any of this, but today you become one of the married. You will have a husband, perhaps children someday, and a home. You'll be far away, and I may not be there to see all that happens in your life, so this is my chance to say I wish you the best, and I'm glad you're my sister."

Tears were flowing by then, and ladies-in-waiting were passing out towelettes to cleanse red eyes. Susannah took her sister by the shoulders and pressed her cheek to her face.

"We will always be sisters, and the distance won't separate us. I won't allow it."

Then the organ vibrated the walls and floor, and with excited voices, the bridal party fell into line and moved toward the grand nave. Flower children had been instructed to drop rose petals from the antechamber all the way up the aisle, and the bride's attendants removed themselves to walk up the aisle one by one, with Susannah following. She met her father at the door, and with tears in her eyes, she took his hand, and they began the long trek to where she could see Simon waiting anxiously at the head of the church.

The Anglican minister was slow and ponderous. His voice intoned the mysteries of marriage for several minutes before turning to Simon and clearing his throat. He spoke the words of betrothal, and the groom repeated his vows in a deep solemn tone. Turning to the bride, the minister repeated his words, with a few changes, and she spoke with calm assurance. The minister pronounced them married and asked Simon if he wished to kiss the bride. There was laughter in the church, as he lifted the veil, failed to get it over her head, and Mary had to step to Susannah's rescue and help roll it over the flowers and ribbons worked into her hair.

After the ceremony, a dinner was held at the home of the bride. It was part of a compromise between the two families. The Clarks were allowed to host the wedding dinner in exchange for the marriage in the Anglican church. Julia Clark had outdone herself, with massive displays of white and yellow chrysanthemums and more than a thousand candles in the house. All the furniture had been removed from the front and back parlors, and multiple tables with white linen covers, red runners, and individual bouquets of red and white roses centered on each one graced the spaces. Each bouquet was wrapped in pale green organza and tied with a ribbon interwoven with gold wire. A staff of fifty had been hired for the celebration, serving lobster bisque, leg of mutton in caper sauce, pork drizzled with apple sauce, oysters on the half shell, braised onions, and French pudding. A live orchestra provided entertainment to the meal, playing tunes ranging from *Camptown Races* and *Molly Do You Love Me?* to *Piano Concerto No. 1 in E Minor* by Anton Rubenstein and *String Quintet No. 7 in G Minor* by Louis Spohr.

They rode away in a carriage bedecked with white ribbons and old shoes, with the dinner attendees throwing handfuls of rose petals over the young couple. They didn't ride far. They spent their first night together in a hotel. Simon insisted on it. He didn't want her to spend her first night with him intimidated by his relations, for which Susannah was grateful.

The first hitch in the evening exposed its fangs as the

coachman drove under the canopy. A man came out to greet them. He had snow white hair and wore the clothes of a Mountain Man: a long buckskin jacket that covered his hips and dark wool trousers, with a plaid shirt whose dominate color was green. He wore beaded moccasins on his feet and a red knitted cap on his head. He stood at attention as the bride and groom stepped from the carriage, then bowed low over the girl's hand, and grabbed the groom around the neck and kissed him on both cheeks.

"You young pup," the man said warmly to Simon. "Introduce me to your bride."

"I didn't expect to see you here, old Ben." Simon laughed, and he seemed especially pleased to see the unusual character. "Susannah, this is Benjamin Claret, the man who taught me to hunt, fish, and track wild animals."

"Mr. Claret, I'm pleased to meet you. I didn't see you at the church." Susannah smiled politely, even as she wondered at the character of the man, to appear in such unusual attire at an elegant hotel.

"Ma'am, I knew I'd be a sore thumb on a finely-polished hand, if I showed up there, but I want to pay my respects. I'll be off, now." He ducked his head, almost in a formal bow, and made to turn when Simon stopped him.

"I must get my wife situated, Ben, but don't leave. We've not seen each other in some time, and I'd like to catch up on our time apart."

Ben agreed to wait, and Simon took his wife by the hand and issued her into the hotel reception area, followed by Ben. Their baggage was brought in by the coachman, who then disappeared with the coach and horses.

Standing in the hotel lobby, Susannah thought she had

never seen anything so grand, even nicer than the church in which they'd been married. Huge crystal chandeliers with a hundred candles, red carpets and drapes, and fresh flowers were everywhere. Simon took her hand, and they crossed to the counter, where he signed their names, then handed her and the baggage to a waiting footman.

"You do understand, Susannah." Simon took her hand before she was whisked away, and he kissed her chastely on the cheek. "This is an old friend, and we won't be long, I'm sure."

"It's our wedding night," she whispered in his ear, as she returned his kiss.

"We have a lifetime together. Ben is an old friend." With an apologetic smile, he disappeared with Benjamin Claret, his friend, into the bar.

Left to her own devices, Susannah followed the footman to the stairs and moved slowly upward, for she was afraid of tripping or stumbling. Their room was large, with a bed and several chairs and tables. There were fresh flowers in the room also, and she was certain that Simon or his father had arranged to have them there. Slightly embarrassed, she pretended to sniff the flowers. They threw off a pleasant, sweet scent. The footman remained for some time, and it was only after he sighed and left that she supposed she should have offered him a gratuity.

Susannah Clark Maxwell crossed to the bed, and spreading her arms wide, flung herself onto the spread and began to weep. She was married! She couldn't believe that she was married to Simon Maxwell, and he had left her to spend the night with his wilderness friend. The pillow became damp with her tears of pity. He didn't want her. He didn't love her. He had married her because her father had forced him. She'd heard it from the servants and from Philip Manning. She'd heard it from her friend, Emily Caruthers. At least, she had thought Emily was her friend. So, it must be true. Even her sister, Alisha had heard the rumor. That had been the purpose of his visit to her house, that fateful day. He was trapped in the marriage by her father, and her own foolishness. Oh, why did she raise her skirts and ask him to remove her shoe and stocking? Why had she believed his false words of love and affection?

She lay on her back gazing at the ceiling, her tears now dry, as she recalled that conversation with Philip Manning at the reception. "You're a fool, Susannah Clark, to marry such a wastrel and liar."

"What do you mean, Philip? Simon is an honorable man. My father likes him."

"Certainly he likes him. He's wealthy and descends from royalty, the rumors say. But, he married you because he was forced into it."

Oh, God, he knew about the shoe and stocking. She looked into Philip's eyes. But, he didn't condemn her. Only her father, it appeared. "What do you mean, Philip?" She repeated the question.

"The rumor is that Maxwell was forced by his father and your father to marry you, or he wouldn't receive his inheritance, which I believe is considerable. His father has written him out of his will, and made his nephew his heir. A clerk in his mercantile store said he overheard the conversation on the day Simon told his father he wanted to go to California. Then, your father told him that unless he married you, he would be disgraced and not be able to practice law in Boston. Your father offered him a good position, but he refused it. He must go to California and begin his own practice there, for he has lost his money and livelihood."

Philip had a gleam of vengeance in his eyes, and Susannah wondered why. Was it because of her sister, Alisha? She'd overheard her father telling a suitor in frank language that he wasn't right for his daughter, but the study door had been closed, and Susannah had fled upstairs rather than be caught eavesdropping. After that day, she'd not seen Philip again at the house. She'd not thought much of it, except for being pleased, as she disapproved of his courting Alisha. Now, she suspected her father had been speaking with Philip that day, and he was currently drunk and wished to make trouble for the younger sister of his frustrated admiration.

She refused to let it bother her on her wedding day, although she remembered another conversation she'd overheard and wondered if there was any truth in the matter.

As she was speaking to Emily Caruthers, Lieutenant Timothy Divine walked by, and with him was Alisha, her sister. Emily sent darts of hatred toward Alisha, and Susannah remarked on her friend's uncharitable attitude. Emily had turned on her and blurted out that she shouldn't be so uppity and certain of herself, for Simon had only married her because his father had cut him out of his inheritance, and he'd been forced to marry her and go to California, for he had no money.

Emily had put her hand to her mouth, shocked at her outburst, and apologized, but the words had been said. Susannah had, of course, forgiven her friend, but the memory was still there. It seemed Philip's tale had become a rumor that had made its way around. Now, gazing at the ceiling, she recalled in great detail the events of that day in her father's library. She remembered that Simon hadn't seemed overly passionate, even when he had professed his love for her. He'd admitted that her father had told him about her disability; so of course, he wasn't shocked when he saw the scars on her deformed ankle and foot. She started crying again and tossed the pillow to the floor. She wished she had the courage to march downstairs and confront him in the hotel bar before the whole drunken lot of callous revelers.

Susannah waited for Simon to come to her, for she was wound up like a child's toy. She wanted to beat him, and kick and scream over the injustice of it all. But, he didn't come, and she knew it was the trapper friend who had caught his attention. She began to calm down and cried herself to sleep, fully dressed in her lovely wedding gown and special shoes.

*****

Sometime later, Simon entered the room cautiously, for he knew that he'd lingered too long with Benjamin, but it was his last chance to see him before they left for New York. He saw Susannah asleep on the bed and crossed the room to her. He could see streaks of dried tears on her cheeks, and her lashes had the remnants of wetness. Her dress was rumpled as though she had tossed around before going to sleep. He raised her skirts and slowly unbuttoned the left shoe, then untied the string on her girdle, and rolled the white cotton stocking over her bruised and scared leg and foot. He removed the right shoe and stocking. He lifted her enough to release the cover beneath her and spread them over her, fully clothed. He felt guilt overwhelm him. He had failed in the first test of their marriage. He'd been so pleased to see Benjamin that he'd forgotten his wife. He leaned over and gently placed a soft butterfly kiss on her tear-stained cheek, and pulling a pillow from the bed, lay on the floor and was soon fast asleep, for it'd been a busy day.

— 17 —

Susannah Maxwell awoke the next morning, alone and still dressed. Her shoes and stockings were gone. She peeked over the side and found them neatly placed beside the bed. She felt gritty, and her face ached from the tears. She climbed from the bed in her awkward manner and put her shoes on without the stockings. She found a looking glass in the water closet and saw her puffy, red eyes. She gasped in horror. Oh God, Simon must have come in and seen her asleep and removed her shoes and stockings, she thought. He must have left in haste, for there was no sign that he'd slept in the room, keeping watch over her in the early hours of morning.

She heard a sound in the other room and knew the time of reckoning had come. She burst angrily through the door prepared to confront him with all she knew, but was stopped in her tracks, for there was a rolling cart with several covered trays. He'd placed a tray of food on a table, and she was so hungry.

She realized she hadn't eaten since the dinner at her father's house. She almost forgave him in exchange for the food, but he turned when he heard her come in, and she saw herself as he must see her: red, puffy eyes, her swollen nose, and wearing a crumpled dress. She'd seen the rosebuds in her hair, sadly wilted, and the wisps of hair had become long, tangled strands. He smiled at her, and her anger boiled up inside. She crossed to stand in front of him and fiercely slapped him across the face. He brought up his hand to the stinging wound and looked at her with shock in his eyes.

"My dear," he began, but he didn't get to finish. Any chance he had for speaking and for apologizing was stolen from him by his wife's ferocious response.

"You are a horrible man. Emily said you were a wastrel, and you'd not want me when the marriage vows were complete. She said you only wanted my dowry, and now she's proved correct."

"But," Simon began, only to face down another tirade.

"I laughed at Philip Manning, thinking his rude comments weren't worth a rebuttal, that he was a gossip monger, and he should quiet his spiteful murmurings. Now, I wish to tell the man that he should shout his truths to the mountaintops. There's nothing about you that's honorable, Simon Maxwell." Susannah's hand had joined her conversation at this point, wagging her finger in his face, and she knew she had gone too far. She was angry and humiliated, and she had no more patience with trying to exhibit control in a situation where her marriage partner had no consideration of her desires and needs. It was unthinkable.

"Can I explain?" Simon tried a smile, only to be lambasted once more.

Susannah let out a stream of curses that would make a dock hand blush. Then, she listed his faults as though she were the prosecutor in a court of law. He remained silent. On and on, for bitter moments, she ranted and raved until she ran out of accusations. She stood and waited, for she expected him to deny the words, but he didn't.

He lifted the metal covers to expose crisp bacon, soft yellow eggs, and various sweet breads, including small, iced cakes. "You must be hungry, dear wife. If you please?"

He held out the chair, and exhausted, Susannah sat down, murmuring, "Thank you." She felt embarrassment warm her neck. He was being kind, after she'd been harsh and cruel. It was almost too much to bear.

"Eggs and bacon?" He gestured to her plate, and when she nodded, he lifted it and gave her one egg and two slices of bacon. He sat himself and put some bacon slices and soft yellow eggs onto his plate. He poured himself a cup of hot coffee after filling her cup.

That did it. She loved to have her coffee early of a morning. After sipping the bitter liquid until it was gone, she poured herself a second cup and drank a sip. It was heaven! She looked at Simon, but he was calmly eating, as though he ate every morning of his life with an angry female.

When they finished, he took the tray, placed it on the cart and rolled it just outside their room. He came back inside and approached her.

"Susannah, my sweet. I wish to apologize." His words were soft, and his eyes were soft. He licked his lips as if he wished to say more, but he didn't know how.

She backed away, not wanting to hear his words. She could think of nothing to say, not after how she'd treated him. She was no longer hungry, but the frustration of the night before wasn't faded completely. It still rankled, and she wanted more than a simple apology. It was her wedding night! She deserved better.

He kept coming, no longer speaking. His eyes said his words for him. He wanted something she wasn't certain she could give, not after last night. He didn't seem to be aware of her hesitations. He lifted her onto the bed, removed her shoes, and then her clothing. She was frightened and tried to keep from shivering. He carried her gently to the water closet, murmuring sweet words of apology into her hair, and set her down on a chair, while he ran hot steaming water in the metal bath tub. He placed several linen towels around the edge so she wouldn't touch the cold metal rim. When the water was nice and warm, he lifted her and placed her in the tub.

"Gently, my sweet. Is your leg okay? I don't want it to pain you." He held her for a moment before setting her into the water.

"Just put me down." Susannah was enjoying the attention, but she was horrified for her disfigured member to be so blatantly on display. No one had seen her so exposed since she was a small girl.

"As you wish." He released her gently into the water, made sure soap and a towel were nearby, then left the room.

Susannah leaned back in the warm water and ruminated on this strange man she'd married. He should be scolding her, yelling, barking, something, but he wasn't. She tried to hear if there were sounds from the other room, but she heard nothing. She reached for the sweet smelling rose-scented soap and washed herself. She looked down at the angry red puckered scars on her left leg. She stretched it out to its greatest length, and placed the right leg beside it. She moaned, as she always did, when she considered the deformity that was thrust upon her in the womb. Why? She asked for the millionth time. Why her? What had happened during her mother's pregnancy that had caused her to be so sadly deformed? As always, there was no answer.

Suddenly, like a bolt of lightning from the sky, she realized that Simon hadn't flinched from her body when he'd seen her unclothed. He hadn't looked with scorn or contempt when he lifted her and carried her to the bath. He was being kind, knowing that she couldn't walk gracefully to the bath. It couldn't be true, the rumors and the slurs against his character. She saw again in her mind's eye the vengeful gleam in Philip Manning's eyes and the crafty, sly glance of Emily Caruthers.

A few moments later, the door opened, and Simon entered. Susannah saw him in a new way. She saw the calm reassurance on his face, the still red mark of her hand, the bold manner in which he reached for the towel and lifted her gently from the tub, holding her steady while she dried herself. He picked her up and took her to the bed. He laid her on the rumpled white flannel sheets, and while she lay watching, he removed his clothes. There was a determined look in his eyes, and she knew not to distract him from his mission. She saw the broad strong shoulders, the slender hips and thighs. She raised her eyes to his face, and he smiled. She opened her arms wide, and he came to her.

— 18 —

Simon's thoughts belied the pleasant and attentive front he presented to his wife. He was angry and disappointed, and he fought to control it. Certainly, spending two hours the previous evening with his old mentor had been a mistake. He saw that now, but he couldn't go back and change it, could he? All the other items on Susannah's agenda she'd thrown up against him? It was as though she was her father, a lawyer presenting a case in a concerted effort to prove him guilty beyond a shadow of a doubt. Why had his lovely bride turned against him? What were the accusations she had flung at his head? Half-lies. Rumors. Gossip. Who had taunted and cleverly planted the ideas of slander against his name and character? He could think of only the man whom he'd seen speaking with her for some length at the reception, and Susannah had admitted as much.

Philip Manning.

Of course, it must be Philip Manning, who was turned away

from his courtship of Alisha, or possibly the sly, clever Emily Caruthers, who was insanely jealous of her sister Alisha, who had captured the charms of Lieutenant Divine. Susannah had brought her name to the argument, also. It was all connected to the sister, both those two complaints, he was certain.

Even as he shunted the blame to the two people he thought most deserving, he acknowledged the slings at his character. The pain of Susannah's accusations hurt him deeply, but he must not allow the bitter jealousy of another person spoil the relationship that had begun to grow between them. He must put them behind him, and try to explain how the truth had been twisted and distorted to make it seem so logical. While she lay beside him on the bed, Simon carefully, and with a strangely calm voice told his wife the truth.

"You laid an accusation against me, my dear, that I've lost my father's love, and his affections are gone to another; and that I can only remain in his good graces if I marry you and leave for lands far from here, never to return."

"Can you say it's not so?"

"My inheritance is mine, alone, from my mother's side of the family. My father has no say in how I spend it, nor has he any control over how I should choose to invest it. My father loves me, and he understands my need to see the western country. It is my desire, and no one has forced my hand in the matter. The decision to make his nephew his heir is purely a practical matter, in case I don't return to Boston."

"Do I understand, then, that this has nothing to do with your character, your transgressions, or your ability to practice law?"

Simon thought his sincerity in telling her the truth was softening her anger toward him. In an attempt to convey his part in the deception of his marriage proposal, he took complete blame, absolving Ezekiel Clark of any part or parcel of the matter from beginning to end.

"I found you attractive from the first meeting at your family's home, when Anthony brought me to meet your family." He said the words sincerely and with conviction. He held her hand and brushed his fingertips against her skin. He wanted her. He did, especially in this very intimate situation, and he hoped to convince her of that. He went on, "I watched you and grew to admire your quick mind as well your lovely face and form. I must admit, I compared you to your sisters Mary and Alisha and found you to be far superior to your siblings in every way. I had only to listen to your mother's serene voice to know that her daughter would act in a similar manner."

"And you could start anew far across the country, with no contacts to provide you a position?" She smiled and stretched, as though she was finding comfort in his words.

"I can practice at my profession and make sure there's always enough to eat and keep a nice home, no matter how humble. I'll try to be a faithful and loving husband, a kind father and a gentleman in all situations, but I will be myself, not some replica or model of deportment thrust upon me by society. If you can't accept my way of life, you must make your decision now, or forever be quiet about it."

Simon Maxwell, having made his confession and statement of independence, rose from the marriage bed, dressed in fresh clean clothes and left Susannah in the bed. He didn't return until nightfall, having spent the day in preparations for their trip to the coast. He left instructions at the reception desk that if the lady in his room chose to leave, that she was to be provided with a coach and horses and coachman to take her to her father's home. He would see to all expenses she incurred while she stayed in the hotel.

— 19 —

It was a very subdued young lady who greeted her husband when he entered their hotel room that evening. Susannah had thought long and hard about her position, and decided that she would remain with Simon. She'd been unkind in her accusations, and had allowed the rumors and jealousy of other people to sway her first opinion of him as a gentleman and leader of men. Now, she understood his character better. But, she decided, he could be free in the restrictions of the marriage bond, for she would see to it. Her natural abhorrence of injustice and power, honed in the experience of her childhood and education in the home of an attorney-at-law, now came to the fore, and she was determined that she wouldn't restrict him in any way. She would find a way to meet each challenge as it presented itself and not judge him or his actions ever again. She would respond to his every command and encourage his adventures in their journey west, even if it meant sacrifice and danger to herself and her children.

Susannah rose from the seat in which she was knitting a scarf for her husband and smiled at him.

"Have you had a profitable day, my husband?" She didn't go to him, as she felt ill-at-ease still, but she was polite, in the manner of a proper wife. If she would do this, it would be done in such a way as to be without fault. Simon would find nothing with which to lay blame against her. He was right, and she was wrong, and she'd not allow herself to think differently.

"Why, yes, wife. I've managed to make much progress in my endeavors. Thank you for your polite enquiries." He was still distant and formal, for which she couldn't blame him. "I see you're still here. Does that tell me you've made a decision on whether to stay in Boston or travel with me into the western wilderness of our country?"

"I judged you harshly and acted the fool today." Her face warmed that he made her say it, but it was her fault. He'd not even spoken harshly to her afterwards. "If you'll hear my words, I would like to beg for your forgiveness for judging you harshly and listening to unwarranted and spiteful gossip. I am quite contrite and at peace with your decision to wander in the wilderness, if that's your desire." She smiled again.

"The matter is put behind us." He seemed to have a load lifted from his shoulders, and he walked to her and hugged her. "Are you hungry? I have reservations at La Belle's and Shells, a restaurant of some repute, if you feel like going out on the town."

"That would be most pleasant." She set her knitting aside, and she dared to take his hand. "I'm sure we'll have a good time, but I must have opportunity to dress. What time are your reservations?"

Susannah put on a long-sleeved, dark-green velvet frock, with a simple hat in gray tied under her chin. Her skirt was filled out around her with three petticoats, and her shoes were well-hidden underneath. She selected a gray umbrella, although it was for decoration, plus it doubled to give her support if her leg grew tired. When she stepped into the main room, Simon had changed into a dark gray, striped coat with wide, turned-up cuffs, and solid trousers over black boots. His top hat was a wide-brimmed affair, and it shimmered in the light.

"My dear." He held out his arm in a touching way, and he smiled at her.

"My dear," she repeated to him, as she wrapped her arm in his, and they left the room in harmony, at least for the moment. Susannah was glad of that, as the day and night since her marriage had been less than pleasant, and she hoped for an improved circumstance.

At the restaurant, they were whisked directly to their table. After a first course of clear duck soup, a course of broiled artichokes in crème sauce preceded the entrée, a curried lamb with white wine. Afterward, the server surprised them with a delicious lemon torte, smothered in meringue and sprinkled with lemon zest.

They walked the streets afterwards, his arm across her shoulders, or her hand nestled in the crook of his arm. They looked into store windows and watched the carriages move slowly down the streets, speculating on where they were going on such a pleasant evening. When the street lamps were fully lighted, with the candles flickering merrily, Susannah remarked on her pleasure in the evening.

"You've made me very happy this evening, Simon. I shall look forward to many more evenings such as this in the future."

She patted his arm and smiled at him.

"This will make a marvelous memory to look back on with fondness in our future years." He nodded sagely but didn't smile when he said it.

"You seem so serious. What can you mean?" They were approaching the hotel, and Susannah stopped him for an answer. "Will we have no more dinners and strolls upon the town?"

"I'm thinking of the howling winds that will surely come through the cracks of our crude cabin in California, or the desert sun as it dries the water holes. I don't wish to worry you, my wife, but to fail to forewarn you would be irresponsible of me. I've heard tales of travelers whose lips were cracked and throats parched, men and women who couldn't be sure they would survive the harsh elements."

"We, though, will be prepared against those dangers, surely. Today, you've organized our trip. If you know of these things, then you must have prepared for them." She put a confident expression on her face, as much to hide the quiver in her stomach, as anything else.

"Aye, trust me, Susannah. Our journey won't be a carriage ride through Boston on the brick streets, but you will be as comfortable as I can make you. I promise you that." He stepped to the door and stood aside as the footman pulled it wide for them to walk through.

"I wasn't worried." She smiled, nodded at the footman, and released Simon's arm to walk through the door. Once inside, they made their way to the stair and began their journey to their room.

*****

"Ah, my dear Susannah. You've finally brought my Simon home to me." Mrs. Maxwell reached a hand to touch Susannah on the shoulder, only pausing for a moment with a noncommittal expression on her face, before moving down the front steps to take both of Simon's hands and welcome him warmly into the house.

Mr. Maxwell stepped to her, saying, "You're part of the family, now, Susannah. You mustn't stand on the street like an urchin." He took her arm and accompanied her up the steps and into the grand residence, as the servants scurried through the door to transport their luggage to their awaiting rooms.

Inside the entrance, standing in a row under the huge crystal chandelier were the kitchen staff and maids. The footman, introduced himself as Franklin, took her cape and gloves and gave a short bow, and turned away. Mr. Maxwell raised an eyebrow her direction and clucked his cheek.

"My dear, as the new daughter of the house, it's only proper that you be acquainted with the household staff. May I introduce Wilhelmina Perry, the housekeeper, Albina, our most excellent cook, Fannie, the upstairs maid, and here is Dolly, the downstairs scullery maid."

As they curtsied and touched the hand she held out to them, she called each by name. She felt uncomfortable at the display, for she knew the Maxwell's were of aristocratic stock and she'd expected to be treated in a proper manner; but she was surprised at the formal introduction. They quickly fled down the hallway, leaving her disconcerted.

She gazed around and found her mother-in-law and husband had left. Her eyes caught a glimpse of the large, gilt framed portraits lining the walls above the winding staircase to the upstairs, and she stood still. Was that a portrait of King George at the head of the stairs? she had time to think, before Jacob Maxwell took her arm and led her toward the drawing room.

"I'm sorry, Father Maxwell. I thought I should wait on my husband, but Mother Maxwell seems to have taken his attention." She was flustered and gave him a quivering smile.

"Nonsense. A mother misses her son, and you'll have him your entire life. You can hardly begrudge her these few weeks until you leave for the western wilderness." He laughed, as if to soften his words.

"Come to me, child." The words echoed from across the hallway, strident and demanding.

"Susannah, my dear, Aunt Sarah would like your presence. You mustn't expect her to await your pleasure." He leaned closer to her ear. "She's very old."

"Of course, Father Maxwell." Brushing at her face, to bring her color up and cover her flustered expression, Susannah headed the direction of the voice, followed by Mr. Maxwell. She stepped through a doorway to find Simon and his mother standing in front of the fireplace, and the elderly aunt poised elegantly on a davenport. Smoke from her elongated smoking stick encircled her head, and she called to Susannah again.

"Now, child," the aunt called, waving her cigarette in the air.

Simon glanced at Susannah, and he nodded at her before turning back to his mother. When Susannah drew close to the aunt, giving a short curtsy, the old woman studied her imperiously.

"Yes, your sisters are much prettier. I told Simon so, but you look like you can bear children, and that's what a wife is

for. Yes, he could do worse than you. A young woman of aristocratic birth would be better, but no one outside of Boston will
notice or care." The aunt sniffed, and she patted the cushion
beside her. "Sit, child. When I visited the Continent as a young
woman . . ."

During her extended time with the Maxwells, Susannah
found the father to be overly proud, the mother weak and timid,
and the aunt entirely too arrogant and demanding for someone
living off another person's charity. The whole atmosphere
seemed inflexible and awkward after living in the casual, loving
environment of her upbringing, where children squabbled over
personal hurts or articles borrowed without asking permission,
and husband and wife showed their affection in public. She
couldn't imagine Jacob Maxwell grabbing his wife Myra from
behind and tickling her ear in front of the children.

During meals, the dining table groaned with good, nutri-
tious food, plenty of fresh milk, butter and cheese. Vegetables
of all kinds were displayed: fish, meat or chicken in abun-
dance. She grew quite fond of the cook and spent time in the
kitchen learning secrets of preservation and baking hints that
would be useful in her new home in the western country. She
learned other beneficial skills, such as carding sheep's fleece
and weaving rugs and blankets. The importance of herbs and
roots gathered in the forest or prairie grassland was made
known to her, and she felt that her education on some points
had been sadly lacking. She could spout Greek verses or Latin
prose with ease, but she didn't know how to wash the linens in
a small amount of water, or make corn fritters or lye soap.

Susannah grew pleased with her time at the Maxwell's, for
what she learned, if not for the generous company. Simon's
daytime hours were monopolized by his mother, his aunt was

too imperious to be borne, and his father far too wrapped up in his own importance to take time for her. She needed the skills the help had to offer, and she would have Simon to herself once they embarked on their journey. She would be patient until then.

— 20 —

Simon was equally busy in those weeks of preparation before leaving Boston. He talked for hours with his friend Benjamin Claret and a few of his former trapper friends about mountain trails, and flooded rivers. The man envied him being able to venture through the western wilderness, but he had demands on him that held him in the East for months, yet, before he could return.

"Ben," he'd called out one day, seeing his old friend walking down the street. Simon rode in an open carriage, with leather seats, black-painted bodywork, and two horses. He had the driver stop. "You must ride with me. I've found new maps of the Lewis and Clark trips."

"Aye, so, my young pup. And where might you have come up with those?" Claret in return hailed his friend with a wave of his arm. His leather leggings were finished in fringe, and his hair was tied in a loose knot at the base of his neck. His shirt was red and green tartan, thick and warm. He wore a light-colored shirt underneath, just visible at the neck. He topped his head with a sewn leather hat with a full brim that sagged around his face. One side was darkened with use, as though Ben regularly grasped it there to remove it at day's end. The other was rolled and pinned with a thick strap and marked with a jaunty feather.

"The library. Come with me. I have transportation, and you have the time, I hope. Your knowledge will help me understand better my upcoming travels west." Simon had few doubts the older man would join him. They'd spoken numerous times in the past weeks, and Ben seemed to be at his leisure and quite pleased to offer his advice on Simon's upcoming travels.

Claret made his way into the carriage, causing it to rock on its long springs. He shut the short door and took the seat opposite Simon. He slipped his leather satchel from his shoulder and dropped it to the floor. Up close, his leggings were nicked and battered. In one place, the leather was holed, and it had been stitched with a thin strip of cording. He leaned forward with his elbows on his knees, with a twinkle in his eyes.

"Real or copy?"

"What do you mean?" Simon suspected he knew. Maps such as those of Lewis and Clark, when reproduced, often carried inaccuracies. It was only in the past few years that photochemical map reproduction had come into general use, and mostly in England or France. In the first half of the century, since the expedition's inauguration in 1804, the greatest portion of the available maps were hand-drawn and inked. If they were the originals or inked close to the time of the expedition's return in 1806, they would serve their purposes well. Later copies might or might not be serviceable, not when details mattered.

"You are the cunning boy." Claret grinned and reclined in his seat, and the carriage moved down the street, jerking over the rough bricks and jostling the riders inside. "The best copies are Lewis' own, made direct from those Clark did in '10. They have an 1814 copy at the library, eh?"

"You've found me out. It's on loan from the Library of Congress. Perhaps we can take afternoon tea afterwards."

They peered over maps and drawings, including those of Captains Meriwether Lewis and William Clark. On following days, Simon rode his horse into the country to practice his skill at rifle and pistol, and twice took Susannah with him, so she, too, could become proficient in the weapons, for she might be called upon to use them to protect herself or the children. He brought home rabbits and wild geese for her to clean and cook. It was very unusual for the family to be in the house kitchens, but Susannah's new friendship with the cook, and the gracious consideration with which she greeted her each time they interacted, gave her access to whatever she needed. She was, of course, considerate not to interrupt meal preparation time, as the many sauces, meats, and vegetables required for the family's meals took precedence over any training Susannah pursued.

His mother and aunt remained stoic throughout the whole time, neither approving nor disapproving of the strange happenings in their midst. They kept to their boudoirs or the parlor, pretending that their social life was more important than the foolish boy's adventure. Simon was forced to decline various social engagements, including afternoon teas with old friends, evening soirees, and a garden party at the Marshall Huguenots' new place on the river. He explained to his mother and his aunt that his upcoming trip consumed all his time, and they must

131

carry on without him.

They were certain he was determined to ruin himself. Simon took their criticisms and conjectures in his stride. At one family dinner, over stuffed quail, asparagus drizzled with honey and maple, and English-style scones, the discussion rose once more.

"Mama, you know I love you, and you've always treated me well, but I'm going west. If I'm unprepared, it will be a disservice to my new wife and those who travel at my side."

"My dear boy," his aunt said, commanding the attention of the dining table. "We traveled west from England, and this is where we landed. Why would you want to go farther? You'll be all alone."

"Auntie, I'll not be alone. I have Susannah." Simon smiled, having found his aunt had trouble remembering his recent marriage. An occasional reminder, and it returned to her once again.

"Who, boy? Oh! How silly of me, the homely Clark child. Yes, she will be the sturdy one, if you can get her to eat more scones. Here, Simon, offer her these." A bowl in the middle of the table held several, and Aunt Sarah pushed the bowl a few inches closer to Susannah.

"Now, Sarah, the girl can ask for the scones if she wishes more. You don't, do you, my dear? I thought not." Jacob Maxwell called to the butler, "Williams, please remove the scones from the table."

Privately, Susannah told Simon that she found the conversations and innuendos to be hurtful and unkind. She would remain polite but distant in their midst, she informed him, for that was the best she could do.

"I'm sure you'll do very well. All I ask, Susannah, is that you entertain Mama's guests with the grace and experience that you learned in your mother's parlor. By the end of your stay, you'll earn their respect and admiration."

"They won't approve of my casual treatment of the servants. There seems to be a strict line between the upper class and the lower class, in their opinion. How can they treat people they see every day with such disdain and contempt?"

"It's only for a few weeks, my dear. Can you stand it that long?" Simon could hardly condemn his family. He'd been brought up with the same attitude, and while not nearly so rigid—Ben Claret was one of his confidants—he didn't consider the servants to be friends. They were employees, only.

At last, the weeks of preparation were complete. Susannah had met with Simon and Ben Claret, once at the park on a particularly sunny day, and another time at a local restaurant, where she became acquainted with her husband's friend and mentor, and discovered the reasons why her husband enjoyed his company. He was engaging and forthcoming with information about their upcoming trip, and she expressed her appreciation to him for the stories he told. She found he had lost a leg due to a bear attack, and a replacement for his crude, hand-fashioned leg was being fashioned for him by a prominent Boston physician. The revelation tweaked her sympathy, and she joined them one day at the library to study the maps of the west and began active participation in the plans to travel to those distant shores.

The day of their departure arrived, and the coach carrying Simon and Susannah Maxwell on the first leg of their journey was at the door. Jacob Maxwell formally shook his son's hand and surprisingly took Susannah into his arms for a hug, telling her he'd grown to appreciate and admire her for her patience and perseverance in the conflicting atmosphere of his home.

Mr. Maxwell held her hands gently in his and said, "I've had the opportunity to visit many times with your father, and I suppose we may become fast friends. We are determined to make the transition from Boston to California easier for you and Simon."

"Your kindness is appreciated." Susannah smiled warmly.

"Thank you, Papa. You've done well. I appreciate your help, and I will correspond regularly. You'll not be left in the dark." Simon placed his hand on his wife's arm, ready to enter the carriage, when Jacob cleared his throat and pulled Simon aside.

"Son, I still have hopes of you starting a trading post or freight line between east and west. If the opportunity provides itself, mind you. Don't chase this for my dream, but let no opportunity go unexplored. Until then, I'll enjoy my dreams in the privacy of my office. Eh, son? We might both benefit from what you find out west."

"I'll keep my eyes out as I establish our new life. I'm certain the shipping companies will send representatives into my office with bills of investment possibilities for me to send back to Boston." Simon smiled and looked away, to see his mother and his aunt giving air kisses to Susannah's cheeks. "I must go, Papa, before Susannah is drowned in love and affection."

Jacob Maxwell sent them off with a promise of writing to them as often as possible to let them know that their mutual families were safe and happy.

— 21 —

The coach stopped for one hour at the home of Ezekiel Clark and his family. The minor children, Raymond and Rufus, clambered over Susannah, and they gathered around Simon, pulling at his arms, calling for information on fierce beasts and wild Indians. They seemed to find the prospect of their sister going off with her new husband to be a great adventure. Simon laughed and told them wicked stories of danger and intrigue that sent the boys from the room with shrieks of alarm.

He called after them, "I'll send you the head of a bison, if I can find one. It's the greatest monster on the American Plains."

They crept back down the stairs, red-faced and laughing. Rufus said his friend's grandfather had a bison head on his wall, and it was very scary, but not that scary. The boys gave Simon a hug, for they had grown fond of him from the time he had first visited their home with Anthony and were sad to see him go from their sight.

"Simon, come into my office." Ezekiel called to his new son-in-law, and when they got inside, several wooden crates rested in the middle of the floor.

"What's this, Father Clark?" Simon suspected he was expected to load these onto the carriage.

"Something you'll make good use of, when establishing your new social position grows tiresome to you. Notice my shelves. I have more display space than before." Ezekiel smiled and indicated a row of shelves just behind his desk.

"Books?" For a moment, Simon thought of Susannah, and her desire to read. Surely, these weren't simple fictions for entertainment. He tried to remember what had been there, and he felt a surge of anticipation. He began to smile as his father-in-law spoke.

"A complete set of law books, bound in leather and in water-tight wrappings. I suspect they'll be in short supply in California, and you have the knowledge and skills to put them to good use."

"Thank you, Father Clark. I'm certain we can find a place in the carriage to convey these along our journey."

"Good. I'll have Jimmie remove them to your carriage. Now, Anthony needs a few moments of your time. He has some words for you."

Anthony was in the back garden, standing among an intricate maze of low-clipped box hedges. A stone, carved bird-bath stood in front of him, with honeysuckle and hummingbirds along the base, and a stone dove rested its feet in the center, its beak tipped down as if readying to take a sip of fresh, cool water. The sun on Simon's back was warm, and his gray and yellow plaid, linen coat, with its wide lime cuffs and thigh-length tails, made him grateful for the shade of the towering trees. Anthony was bareheaded, with his hair slicked and pulled to the sides, with a part in the center.

"Anthony!" Simon called to him, with his hand high in the air.

"Ah, so my father has turned you loose." Anthony smiled. "Come see this, my friend. You'll find it interesting."

In the bird bath, a half-dozen tadpoles swam. Anthony placed his finger in the water, and one came up to nibble against his skin.

"A project?" Simon chuckled.

"This is Raymond's doing. He comes every day to add water. Look, one is already growing legs."

Sure enough, one of the small creatures had two little nubs at the base of its tail. Its tail was also shorter than the rest, already being absorbed into its body to provide nutrients for the growth of its legs.

"I remember you and I doing this very thing several years back." Simon watched the little scene warmly. It was a connection to a time from long ago, a door that in minutes was to be closed forever. "Has Rufus seen this?"

"And declared himself fully uninterested." Anthony chuckled. "He'll become interested once again when the frogs are large enough to put down his sister's dress. Papa showed you the books?"

"He did." Simon chuckled. "And he's volunteered to send them with us."

"You'll find them useful, I'm sure."

"I'll be establishing my residence, and perhaps exploring the wilderness. There are no great cities to be found in California, not like Boston. My legal skills may be of doubtful benefit to me for a time." Simon wondered that no one seemed to take him seriously, not even his good friend.

"Having a career to fall back on is never a bad thing. You may rejoice one day you can return to the law." Anthony turned his head and gave Simon a quick look before glancing away.

"I fully intend to. I never meant to drive us apart, my friend." Simon saw the distance from his friend in the man's eyes, and he hated it, for the previous, casual relationship between them in their college years was gone forever. It was a regret that he would carry with him across the continent, but he couldn't regret his marriage, for he had found a sort of peace with his decision to travel his own road in life, unrestricted by the boundaries of society or dictates of parental forces.

"You've been my closest friend, and I'll miss you immensely." Anthony continued to toy with the tadpoles, and he didn't look up.

"As I will you. I must go, now. A hand of well wishing?" Simon offered his hand just to where Anthony could see it.

The man took a deep breath, looked at the hand, and wrapped it in his own. Then, with a sudden movement, he wrapped his arm around Simon and wished him well in his travels. Simon returned the heartfelt farewell, telling Anthony that he hoped him much success in his career as a lawyer, and that he was certain he would succeed, for his family loved him and would support him in all that he did.

Simon walked the path through the hedges, not looking back. His life was ahead of him, in California, with his wife and the land he hoped to acquire. When he stepped through the door, he found Susannah surrounded with her siblings. She was laughing, and he couldn't help but smile. This was a good memory for her to store away, for their trip would be long.

— 22 —

After having spent many hours researching traveling by private coach, railroad, steamship, horseback and donkey cart, and being made well-aware of the hardships they might face along the way, the couple was glad to be apprised of a ship leaving for California in a fortnight. It would be departing from New York, and Simon used his education and wealth to the best advantage to assure accommodations as comfortable as he could for Susannah. He praised God every night that she wasn't with child, for the rough seas they would assuredly face and the depredations of life aboard ship would be unbearable with the addition of an uncertain illness. The relationship at best hadn't been an easy one, for he still harbored a resentment of her suspicions and accusations against his character and integrity, and she missed the love of her many family members and acquaintances. She'd never been without the company of other people, both young and old, and she now had only Simon for her source of mental stimulation and physical guidance.

The baggage that he thought necessary for them to have aboard the ship encompassed various items, most importantly her precious shoes and boots, for several times they had to lighten the load, deciding the items they would no longer be shipping by wagon. To save time in passage, Simon decided the Isthmus overland passage was the best option, for stories persisted of sickened passengers who took the Cape Horn route. They packed carefully, to prevent lost items at railroad terminals, or unsecured gear being stolen by thieves in the night. Food might become a major source of trouble while in Panama. But, Simon wasn't discouraged nor disheartened, and he spoke to the captain of the ship to ensure that when they reached Panama, they would disembark adequately stocked with plentiful food of hearty and filling substance. Searching for a contact for traversing Panama overland, he scoured the streets of the city until he uncovered news of a businessman with information about portaging his luggage and other belongings from the Atlantic shore to the Pacific. He gave his source a small silver coin for his trouble.

At the place of business, Simon offered the clerk at the desk his card. Upon meeting the proprietor of the establishment, the man told him there were several options for crossing the land bridge between east and west. He apologized that the Panama railway wasn't yet completed, but there were paddlewheel steamers. The worst part of the journey would be the fifty-mile overland trek through the jungle. They would first arrive at the Island of Manzanillo on the Atlantic side, cross the country, and resume their water-borne journey from Panama City on the Pacific. He could certainly set up overland transport before Simon left from New York, but he couldn't guarantee it, and Simon would do as well to hire porters once he arrived. He offered the name of his business affiliate in Panama, and said he would wire the man in advance of Simon's arrival. Simon thanked him for his time, they agreed on a mutual price for his services and Simon departed for his hotel.

Simon and Susannah's ship sailed from New York on a wet and dreary day. They had good quarters on a whaler heading to the southern waters. It was delivering supplies for the new railway just breaking ground on Manzanillo and would unload at Panama before continuing south. Simon bargained for the captain's quarters, and he agreed to pay a premium for the extra space. The low, beamed ceiling was spacious enough, with a built-in bed, which Simon had outfitted with a new mattress and fresh bedding. Susannah measured the windows across the back of the vessel, and she brought cloth to make curtains to improve the space. A wood-burning stove was in one corner to heat the room, but the captain assured them the weather would warm as they traveled south, and he was certain it wouldn't be used.

The days at sea were long and languorous, and Simon spent his time learning the ins and outs of the sailing craft, while Susannah wrote letters, improved her sewing skills, and walked the deck twice a day to relieve the tedium of the tight and dark spaces.

Their arrival on Manzanillo was a welcome relief. The wharfs led to a city just under construction, which was named Aspinwall by the English-speaking community, while the city's Spanish residents called it Colón. The local infrastructure was totally lacking and suffered in convenience and comfort, but Simon did manage to secure lodgings in a hotel that was clean and respectable. After their evening meal the first day, Simon walked to the temporary offices of the transportation company recommended to him in New York. He wore a suit and black string tie, his boots were shined, his face clean shaved, his hair neatly combed. Several immigrants were standing outside the building talking, chewing tobacco or smoking a pipe. One man had what looked like a small cigarillo. He was dressed in a more modern fashion than the others around him, although he seemed to have no regard to color scheme, for he wore a pair of dark brown trousers, a homespun blue plaid shirt almost hidden by a red tweed jacket, and his boots were a scuffed brown. He was clean shaved and had friendly gray eyes. Simon asked if this was the location where he could find out more about porters and obtaining space on a paddlewheel steamship to the Pacific coast, as his contact in New York was to have sent a wire for them to be expecting him.

"Aye, the man you want to see's inside. Don't know about no contacts from New York, but mebbe there's been." The man took a large drag from his cigarillo, and blew the smoke around his head in a circular motion. "Best get in there quick; the porters are being claimed fast."

Taking his advice seriously, Simon made his way into the building, leaving the door wide behind him. There were three men in the room: one sat behind a table and seemed to be in authority; one was arguing with him; and the other man stood between Simon and the table, apparently waiting his turn to speak with the clerk.

Simon couldn't help hearing the argument between the men. The businessman was telling the other that he couldn't get porters without transferring funds to the company account to ensure they would be paid, as well as provided meals for the trip overland. For anything personal, he could buy supplies at Panama City, if he had the money, but he wasn't going with the larger party without an adequate amount of supplies for his personal group. The immigrant asked if he needed a wagon, for he was a single man. All he wanted was a pack mule to carry what he would need.

The leader came back at him with the same answer as though he'd repeated it many times in the last few weeks, that the people who joined his party must be able to provide for themselves. No one would provide charity to a stranger who ran out of supplies halfway to Panama City. The man started to say something in reply, then with a sound of disgust, turned and left the building, rubbing against the other stranger. The second man left with him. Simon heard a sigh of regret and anger from him as he passed by.

Simon supposed that meant it was his turn, as there was no one left inside. The man looked up and gave him a searching gaze. He looked back down and scribbled something on a paper in front of him, then took out a small knife and sharpened his quill pen point.

Simon waited patiently as he'd been taught in his college classrooms. "Never speak unless spoken to by the man in authority," he'd been told by one of his professors. He didn't let his eyes drift from side to side or away from the man's pen knife. He was concentrating on the process of sharpening a pen, and he almost missed the man's voice when he spoke.

"Name?" barked the leader. He continued with his sharpening of the pen. Simon was afraid he would cut his finger when he looked up at him, knife still working.

"Simon Maxwell." He said nothing else, for he'd been asked nothing more. He looked the man in the eyes and liked what he saw. There was honesty and determination in his eyes.

"Farmer?" The man finally laid down his knife but kept the

pen in his hand.

"No, sir, lawyer, but I could become a farmer, for a time, or possibly an explorer. I wish to get overland to make my ship to California. My man in New York was to notify you of my arrival." That seemed to catch the man's attention.

"Nothing's come through to me, but then, with the construction all around, news is sometimes slow. You, though. Lawyer, you say? Where you from? What makes you think you could become a farmer?"

Simon saw the puzzle in his eyes. "I'm from Boston, in Massachusetts, sir. I've studied for the last six years to become a lawyer, but I'll be new to California and am unsure how long it will take me to get established. I expect I'll do what's necessary until I get my practice on a stable footing. For a time, I'll be satisfied hunting or fishing, or walking behind a plow, if necessary. The confinement of an office or courtroom will come in its time."

There was such passion in his answer that the man seemed taken aback. He cleared his throat. "I've seen hundreds of men cross in front of me the last few weeks since my return from Panama City, securing wagons, carpenters and wheelwrights for the trip overland, but you're my first lawyer. Panama needs trained lawyers, if you've a mind to make your home here. Will you consider it?"

"No, sir. I need to find someone who might transport my baggage overland. I'm married, and I've secured passage on board the *Scottish Clipper* for the journey by sea. I felt it would be an undue hardship for my wife to travel by wagon from New York all the way to California, and the same is true here. I understand there's the possibility of a steamship passage part of the way through the jungle."

"Ah, aboard a vessel, 'tis one way to go. Many choose the water route, however, there are few vessels with a private cabin. Since you're married, any children?"

"I'm only recently married, sir. No children."

"And there's no chance you might make your home in Panama?" The man didn't really look hopeful, more like he felt he needed to ask, or had been told to ask. He sighed, "But, you're right; it can't be a very lucrative business among a valley of farmers." He looked more closely at Simon's dress and manner. "You appear to be a city fellow. You have much to transport?"

The questions came in rapid fire order, much as Simon would have done to a witness in the chair before a judge and jury. Simon didn't flinch or stray from the subject when asked with superfluous answers that were unimportant to the question.

The man questioning him remarked, "I've known a few lawyers, good and bad, in my time, and keeping your private business private is a good trait to have among a flock of shifty farmers and stock herders." He chuckled as he searched through his stack of papers until he found the one he wanted and looked at it for a few moments.

Simon didn't shift from his place, letting the comments go as idle talk from a man who saw all sorts stand before him. Only Simon's eyes moved, following the man's hands. He looked up at Simon, paper in hand.

"Got a promissory note from a fellow traveler. He made it to Panama, hoping to get passage from Panama City, but his wife and children died, and he can't afford his passage home. Invested in a barge moored on the Chagres he might be willing to sell cheap to someone wanting to travel by steamship. He's borrowing money to stay in a hotel; will go broke before long if he doesn't find passage out of here. If you've got a bit of money on you, you could hire his team of mules for the over-land portion of the trip, even buy the barge, though don't know if you'd be able to resell it. He might even drive the mules for passage on the steamship. He needs the money bad."

"How many mules, sir?" Simon felt excitement swell inside. "Is it far to the steamship?"

The man laughed. "It's a few miles along the Camino Real to the Chagres River, then by barge to Cruces. It's possible to make an overland passage, but if you wish luxury, then the steamship is the way to go. In Cruces is where your long journey begins."

"Can you assure me the mules are fit and able to make the trip?" Simon wouldn't commit himself until he had discussed the matter further. "How much time do I have to fill the rest of the supply list and work with the team?"

"It would be best to start now. With good timing, you should meet your ship for California in plenty of time."

"That would be fine. I suppose I've time to find an additional driver, although I can't put it off for long. We're at the Royal George Inn, room four."

"Royal George, huh?" The man grinned. "After one of them English kings."

"I didn't like the name at first. My aunt would choke on her morning tea, if she knew I was staying at an English-style hotel. She's British, you see. The 1812 War." Finally, Simon Maxwell felt comfortable enough in the man's presence to give out a little information.

"Your aunt traveling with you? I'd like to meet this British aunt who'd choke at the sound of an inn named for an English king because of the result of the war."

"Nah. My aunt has remained behind in Boston." Simon

shrugged, paying it no more mind.

The man wrote out instruction on where he would find the mules for their driver to load Simon's supplies. He drew a crude map for his man to show how to locate the barges, then rose and shook hands. He told Simon he was well pleased with the conversation. Lawyer or farmer, he was certain the man would make his mark in the western country of the northern continent.

— 23 —

Outside the building, Simon found the same men who seemed to be hanging about. The one with the cigarillo moved to join Simon at his carriage. He paused a moment, then spoke, as Simon was about to mount the carriage steps.

"You get a driver to portage your things?"

"We discussed the matter." Again, he started to walk away, but Cigarillo detained him.

"Mind if I join you for a few moments?"

Simon wasn't usually a suspicious man, but his training and natural instincts were awakened. He nodded his head. It could be seen as a positive or negative, but the man decided it was a positive and joined him.

The two men walked for some minutes in silence, and then Cigarillo burst out, "Name's Schmidt. Howland Schmidt; came from Maine. Not the part of Maine near the ocean, but inland in the tall trees. I heard about the giant trees in California. Some as big as a house, they say, and so tall a man can't see the top, standing on the ground."

Simon looked at him strangely, for Benjamin Claret had told him the same thing. Had seen them himself, he said. The man, Schmidt, went on.

"Have this idea in my head to start a lumber mill, harvest some of those trees, for the settlers going to the gold fields'll need logs and building material for houses, furniture and barns. The thing is, ran out of money once I got to Panama. Met with the local authorities, and was told that if I can find someone to go in with me as a partner, I might get enough porters to move my equipment to Panama City. Got a wife and two children, ages three and five, and can't afford to linger much longer at the hotel where we're staying. Got to either get across this mosquito-infested land or find a way to make it back to Maine."

"You have a team and wagon?" Simon used his training to get more answers, refusing to make a decision before he could determine what the man wanted from him. Was he asking to be made his partner? Or, was he asking for money outright?

"I tried to buy one when we arrived a few weeks ago, but would have had to sell it at the paddleboat docks. Got a steam-powered milling saw I couldn't sell, most of my tools left and a strong back, and am willing to work for my wages."

"Can you manage a team of six or eight mules?"

"Could maybe manage four or maybe six, but eight would be too many, except in the high mountains. It depends on the size and weight of the load. Did the clerk inside tell you about the barge for sale?"

"He did. My wife and I are continuing by sea, but we must get overland, first." Ideas were percolating in Simon's head. If this man desired to join his portage team, and he could transport his and Susannah's belongings, there might be a deal to be worked here. "Tell me, sir, more about your lumber milling equipment and what it would take to get it to the far shores. I think the milling saw would be your bulkiest item."

It turned out that the steam-powered saw was disassembled and in crates; and Schmidt wished to introduce him to another man who might get his milling supplies and Simon's possessions to Panama City, and possibly on to California from there. Simon stopped near a sturdy wagon, and Schmidt stopped with him. He saw a gray-headed man step from a door. The man was dressed in the manner of a farmer, homespun shirt and loose trousers. He had a black felt hat on his head. He stepped closer to Simon and Schmidt.

"Hello, may I help you?" The man's voice was gruff, and Simon could see that there had been recent tears, for his eyes were red-rimmed and puffy, else the man was drunk. He would soon know for certain.

"Yes, I was told I could hire you. What are you asking for taking this man's milling equipment to Panama City, along with some of my personal luggage? I have need to hire a number of mules for the job." Simon stood looking at the wagon as the man framed his answer.

"Got six fine mules, although horses might get you there, instead. If you want the mules, that would add to the price of the deal. How much you offering for me to travel so far? You didn't say."

"We would have to strike a fair bargain. Do you mind if I look around some? Where are the mules?" The man's speech pattern was odd to him, but he considered the words clear and sharp, so the man wasn't drunk.

The man pointed to a spot under a clump of trees where

about a dozen mules were happily chomping on the grass. Taking his answer as permission to look over the man's things, Simon walked that direction. He circled the supplies. The two men followed his every move, stepping back when he withdrew to another place. No one said a word but allowed him room for his inspection. He moved off sharply toward the mules and asked the man which were his own. They were pointed out to him and he inspected the teeth, withers, ankles and legs to see if there were sores or blemishes. Having completed his tour, he turned to the man. Schmidt was hanging on his every word, and Simon wondered what he was thinking.

"Are you including the harness and farming supplies in your price?" He could see the man hesitate. Simon had seen desperate men before and knew the man wanted as much money as possible, perhaps to fund feed or board for the animals. Simon felt a sort of pity for the man. He must have had dreams of glory, such as his own, but had lost the desire for land in California.

"Same price, don't have much food left. Got some tools, a grinding stone and an extra wheel."

Simon could see the pain in the man's eyes to have to settle for such a small price for the items. Still, the man inside had gotten him to thinking. Simon wasn't a farmer, but he would have to do something when he first arrived in his new home, and this was a good backup plan, if it panned out. "What kind of tools?"

"Blacksmith tools, hammer, tongs, forge. I can take 'em along and let you have them, if you want to hire the mules."

Simon couldn't believe the man was willing to let such items go for such a cheap price; why, those items alone were worth the two hundred to an experienced blacksmith.

"What's your name?" Simon thought to ask, for he wanted to know more about this man willing to sacrifice his most valuable possessions to make his way back home.

"James Townsend. Came from Vermont. My grandfather was with Ethan Allen and the Green Mountain Boys at Fort Ticonderoga," he said with some pride, then shrugged. "But, the county's getting crowded. Too many people, and not much land, with the old men leaving it to their sons."

"Is that what happened to you? Are you a younger son and the older got the property? Are you determined to go back to Vermont?" Simon could hear some bitterness in his tone.

James Townsend's posture changed, as though surprised by the questions. "Surprised to find a stranger can know so much about my position in life. I'm the fourth in line, after my three older brothers. My father gave me a hundred acres, but that's not much to grow wheat, oats, barley and rye. In Oregon, they say a married man can get 640 acres, or a single man 320 acres free if he builds a cabin and plants a crop. Sounded like a wonderful idea when I told the missus, but she and the child died, and now I can't get back. Thought if I invested in a barge, I could earn the money, but even that's been a bust." Tears filled his eyes and he ducked his head, wiping his face with the backs of his hands.

That settled the matter for Simon Maxwell. "You got a particular reason to go to Oregon, besides the free land? Would you be willing to go to California?"

"California? To the gold country?"

"I'll tell you what I'll do, Mr. Townsend. I'll buy the team of mules, blacksmith tools and grinding stone for three hundred dollars, or give you one hundred dollars for the same items and a job as my portage team leader, if you'll pick up this man's milling equipment and carry my personal effects to Panama City for my wife and me. I'll even purchase your barge for that portion of the passage for fifty dollars, and if it can be resold, we'll divide the profit. We might work a deal for California after that, if you serve me well. Which would you rather do?"

Schmidt raised an eyebrow, and rubbed a bit of sand from his eye. "I must say, sir, I'm stunned at your unexpected generosity. I'd seen something in you at the entrance to the place of business and thought you might be willing to help me in my own situation, but never thought you'd take a chance like this on a complete stranger's word alone."

James Townsend dropped on his knees before Simon and kissed his hand. In some kind of blubbering, stammering language, he thanked him, promised loyalty and obedience to his dying day, if he would let him make his way to California. There in the shade of the trees, with no one to hear but Howland Schmidt and Simon Maxwell, he told them of his fear and humiliation if he had to return and beg his older brother for assistance. His brother was a tyrant and ruled over the family with a hard hand. But, he'd seen no other way to proceed after his wife died.

Simon heard him out and helped him to his feet. He was truly humbled and had never thought it would come to this when he'd walked to see the wagon and mule team. He looked at James Townsend with a sharp, fierce look.

"Mr. Townsend, never do that again. I'm a man, like yourself. I'm not a lord of the realm, nor am I an overseer of slaves. If you wish to work for me, you'll treat me as an equal, and when we arrive in California, you'll file your claim to the land, as I will. I'll pay you the going rate for a portage team leader, and if you choose to sell your mules and leave the country, your sales price can be used to purchase additional supplies you need." Simon waited a moment to see that his edict was understood, shook hands with Townsend and walked with Schmidt back to his carriage.

As a lawyer, he thought he'd handled the deal with generosity and legal expertise, but, as a man, he wasn't so sure. Had he made a mistake to take on James Townsend as an employee? Was he adding a burden to Susannah's life that she wouldn't approve? What would she have done in similar circumstances, if she were a lawyer? He would ask her tonight in the privacy of their room at the hotel. For now, he had to consider the matter of Schmidt, who clung to him like a leech. What to do? His idea of a sawmill was sound, but he had a wife and two young children. Would the company of another woman and small children once they reached California make Susannah more agreeable to their marriage? Simon knew with regret that Susannah missed the members of her large family. He'd noted that she often stared into space and seemed to be withdrawn from him. A few yards from the parked rental carriage, he turned and spoke to Schmidt.

"Schmidt, I wish that you hadn't witnessed that scene with Townsend today, but things happen as they should. You may have noted that I'm a lawyer by trade, experienced in matters of a monetary nature and deeds, wills and business contracts. You've told me a part of the circumstances in which you've found yourself. You said that you can get your supplies and equipment across the country, if you can find a partner in the business of lumber and timber. I'm willing to become your partner on certain conditions." He stopped speaking. He could see that Schmidt was interested, but the man was quiet, as if waiting to hear the conditions set down for such a partnership. "Well, man?"

"I appreciate the offer, sir, but I'm sure I can't expect such a generous offer as you extended to Townsend. If you still wish to purchase my milling equipment, my offer still stands." The carriage horse seemed restless, and Simon calmed him with a hand on his nose and bridle.

"You say you have a wife and children?"

Schmidt nodded in the affirmative.

"Very well." Simon wondered if he was making another mistake. He wished he'd time to speak to Susannah before leaping into another unchartered course of action that might be to her detriment. "I know nothing of your end of the timber and lumber business. I'm a city man, where a person simply goes to the lumber yard and buys what he needs." He chuckled at the idea of himself buying lumber, for he'd never owned anything in which he needed lumber before. "But, I can see the huge potential of a sawmill in California. I visualize hundreds, maybe thousands of immigrants coming from the eastern United States, seeking gold, but surely most of those miners will remain in the new state. All of those families will need homes and furniture and barns, as you said. I don't know how many houses or barns can be built with the timber on that land. I'll leave such matters and details to you." He drew a deep breath, and noticed that Schmidt had become tense and watchful.

"I'm willing to finance your trip across Panama and the oceans to California, whatever you need, wagons, mules or oxen, supplies, foodstuff and clothing for your family. I'll help you with setting up your sawmill for one year, after which you're on your own, profit or loss. All I require in exchange is thirty percent of the profit for the first year; seventy percent will be your own. It will be a simple business proposition between you and me. If there's another lawyer on the train, he can set up the legal papers; if not I'll write them and make sure that you understand the terms of the contract, along with several witnesses.

"Now, here is, as they say, the stinger, the condition to which I need your agreement. You must portage with Townsend, so that my wife and my things are secure in this foreign country. This will be a secret between us. If your family fails to get along with Townsend, please feel free to withdraw from the situation at any time. I won't hold it against you or your wife. Sometimes, people simply cannot remain friends even when they wish it."

Simon looked into the distant horizon, remembering the closeness between himself and Anthony Clark, now lost forever, and the cruelty of Philip Manning and Emily Caruthers. He cleared his throat.

"This matter of the condition in no way has any effect on the business contract. It'll remain intact unless either party wishes to break it. There'll be no penalty."

Schmidt stammered and spoke with a burr in his voice. "I understand why James Townsend wanted to bow and kiss the hand of such a generous man. A deal of thirty percent to seventy percent is a magnanimous offer of kindness, almost charity, in fact. And to help me for the first year is beyond what I could have believed possible. My wife, Alice, has worried herself almost sick in the last few weeks as our supplies have dwindled, and our money has run low."

"Man, don't go soft on me." Simon sighed. He was offering a business deal, one that would benefit him, as well. It wasn't charity.

"Sir, I cannot believe that you would trust the word of a

stranger so quickly, first Townsend, and then myself. What if I were a wastrel and scoundrel, out to rob you of your money? I thank you from the bottom of my heart, and my wife will thank you, as well. We'll do what is in our power to help you bring comfort and solace to your wife in her present circumstances. And, if the business fails, I'll hold myself totally to blame, for it's a very generous offer; one that I couldn't have dreamed possible yesterday. Truly, it was a divine inspiration when I saw you at the entrance of the tent and forced my attentions to your notice. Thank you."

Again, that feeling of humility and guilt passed over Simon as he saw the delight in the eyes of this stranger. Had Ezekiel Clark been right? Had his father seen something Simon couldn't see? Was it his mission and his duty to help others along the path of trouble and sorrow? He'd thought his law training a waste of time and effort, when he would much rather be following in the footsteps of his friend Benjamin Claret. Maybe, California was his destiny, not only as an explorer, but as a lawyer as well. How Anthony would laugh at such vanity. He'd best get on with his own trouble and let others do the same. Or was he playing the fool?

To cover his emotional turmoil, Simon pretended to check the harness of his horse, turned and plodded up the steps and into the office of Arthur Stoner, the portage clerk. They waited patiently until he had finished with his other business, then explained the contract between themselves, and Simon told him of the agreement made with James Townsend.

The clerk put on his solemn face while he listened to the two men. After the deal was done, he pulled Simon aside and told him he'd seen such agreements settled at the start of a trail across the Isthmus come to naught too many times to think that these would succeed, but it certainly settled some of the problems that he'd encountered the last weeks of the planning for the trip.

— 24 —

Simon walked the short distance to the hotel in which he was staying. He felt mixed emotions. On the one hand, he felt that he'd done the right thing, but doubts and worries assailed him as he climbed the steps to the room he shared with Susannah. He found she had spent the morning looking through the local newspapers, although only one had been in English. She told him she knew none of the people mentioned in the articles, nor was she particularly interested in the politics of Panama, but it had kept her entertained for a while. She had brought out her sewing basket and hemmed a few handkerchiefs, but that wasn't satisfying either.

She called for tea in the early afternoon and pretended that she was enjoying it with her mother and Alisha. Simon thought it a good time to tell her his news, and he joined her for tea. He poured himself a tepid cup of the sweet brew and sat down after greeting her with a light kiss on the forehead. He asked how her day had gone, and could tell that it hadn't gone well. She talked for some moments about the local politics, what she had been able to make out in the English newspaper she had found. There were stories of the gold fields, and the ships abandoned in San Francisco harbor, and one article about a man who had been hanged for stealing a claim. She stopped speaking when she saw that his attention had wandered.

"My dear, I may have done something today of which you don't approve." Simon felt his way through the process of explaining his news.

"Yes, my husband?" Susannah had finished her tea. She smiled and looked at him expectantly. "This is a surprise. You don't usually include me in your schemes and plans."

"I went to the business of a man who could set us up with a team of porters to manage our belongings across to the other side of the Isthmus. He seems a good man and I'm sure will be a good leader on the way to California. He told me of a farmer whose wife had recently died and he wished to return to Vermont. The man wanted to sell his team of mules." He saw that he had Susannah's attention, so continued. "As I was leaving the building, a man who was smoking one of the new types of cigarillos stopped me and walked with me."

Susannah accepted the explanation with no comment.

"He said his name was Howland Schmidt and he planned to build a sawmill in California, where there's rumored many forests with large trees. He's from the state of Maine and in the timber and lumber business. We walked together for a time. Along the way, Schmidt told me more about his situation. He has a wife and two small children. They're staying at a hotel, as are we, preparing to move overland to meet the boats. The thing is, my dear; I'm now his partner."

"What do you mean, partner?" Susannah brightened. "I'm sure there must be more."

"I've agreed to lend him the money for supplies and mules, to travel to California, in exchange for thirty percent of the timber production when he has his business working properly."

"Only thirty percent? But, that's hardly enough to pay the expenses of the enterprise. We have to build a house and start your new law practice . . ."

"That's the idea, darling. He'll fell the trees, haul the logs and help build our house. I'll insist that we have a shelter before winter sets in. We may have to build a communal building of sorts, with several families living together, if we get to California too late to construct individual cabins. But, he claims that he's an experienced timber man. There's half our problem solved, for I'm sure I wouldn't know the first thing about cutting logs in half. Benjamin taught me the rudiments of building a cabin with either logs or mud bricks, but to have Schmidt do it for us would be a blessing, don't you see?"

"To spend so much time with strangers frightens me. Do you think we'll have to live with other families for the first winter?"

Simon wasn't surprised that his wife had caught that part of his story. She was shy in many ways. She'd been trained in the social graces by her mother and father, but to live in a log cabin or sod house with strangers would be a challenge he hoped she didn't face, although they must be realistic.

"My dear, it won't be so much different than living in a hotel, will it? Except that there are walls between the rooms and a bath house?"

"Yes, as you say, it'll not be so different, and we'll soon be sleeping aboard a ship, which my mother would frown upon,

161

I'm sure. The walls are so thin a person can hear a conversation between rooms." Her natural humor restored, she started to rise and get her shawl, for the temperature seemed cooler, but he stayed her with a hand.

"That isn't all my news, dear. You haven't noticed that I said I was on my way to talk to a man about buying his wagon and mules." There was a twinkle in his eyes.

"I can think of nothing worse than living with strangers and possibly animals in the same room." She smiled. "Yet, I suppose I must also prepare myself for other disasters and dangers."

"You are such a dear." Simon kissed her on the forehead. "The man's name is James Townsend. His wife recently died. He came from a family where the father left most of the property to the older son, with the younger ones receiving only a stipend. You've seen the thing many times I'm sure, in your father's practice. He received one hundred acres of land, only enough to support a small family. He heard of the free land in Oregon. As a married man, he would receive 640 acres. That was his dream. It would be a great humiliation to go back to the older brother and beg for mercy, hoping to receive the hundred acres he shunned before. Can you see that, dear?"

"You've bought his team of mules, then, to help him on his way back to Vermont? That is a nice gesture, otherwise, he might never find his way home."

"But, I've done more than that, Susannah. I've given him a job."

"A job? At what, pray tell?" Susannah set her tea cup aside, and it shook in her hand.

"Why, as driver of the same team of mules that I have purchased from him."

"Oh, Simon, but how humiliating to be driving the team that one once owned. How could you treat the man so cruelly? But, wasn't he going to Oregon? We're going to California; and he's agreed to go there?" Susannah shook her head sadly.

"But, he didn't think I was treating him cruelly. He bowed on his knees before me and kissed my hand, he was so overcome with gratitude that he didn't have to return to his tyrant of a brother and beg for succor."

Susannah's eyed grew round and startled. "I cannot visualize a man prone on the ground, kissing the hand of my husband for such a cruel turn."

"You see, Susannah, I gave him the choice. He was asking two hundred dollars for his possessions, when they're at least worth four hundred. He didn't realize the worth of the objects he had. He not only has the wagon and six mules, but a blacksmith's tools and farming equipment, although I didn't buy those, and a grinding stone and so many other small things that we need ourselves to use in California. I offered him three hundred dollars cash, or one hundred dollars and a job. He took the job."

"More than he asked? And he turned it down?" She looked out the window, let her eyes rest on her tea cup, and looked back to Simon.

"Darling, to a man, a job is worth more than a large sum of money at hand. It means security for the future; it means a regular wage that will last over time; and if a man is thrifty, one can accumulate that large sum of money. If he's a decent, honest man, he won't see the humiliation of driving the wagon he once owned; he'll see the future life he'll live when he arrives in California, with a sum of money that he has earned in his pockets, and the hope of that land that is promised. It will give

163

him dignity and a sense of self-worth that he wouldn't have if he returned to his brother's home. And, he'll have enough money to go on to Oregon, if he finds that California isn't to his advantage. Can you not see that?"

"I suppose you're right, for I've seen men in my father's office reduced to begging for pennies, when they've once owned dollars. I will withhold judgment until I can see more of the man's character, for if he's to drive our mules, I'll know him well once we're in California." She rose from her seat.

"I'm right. You'll see." Simon rose to join her.

"My dear, I'm sure you know what's best to be done. My father said that a woman cannot understand the ways of a man, and I've found him to be very wise. I'll accept your solutions to the many problems at hand. For you're very wise, also." She rose on her toes and kissed his cheek, and then smiled that crooked smile that he loved.

He took her in his arms, and she melted into his embrace.

— 25 —

Three days later, a knock came at the door of Room 4 in the Royal George Hotel, and Susannah moved to answer it. Standing in the hallway were two ladies and two small children, a boy and a girl. She bid them enter, then stood aside and closed the door. One of the ladies was tall, slender and middle-aged, with gray hair and brown eyes. The other was much younger, about twenty with blond curls and freckles. The younger seemed to be the dominant character of the two. She told the children to sit on the floor and be still, when Susannah hadn't even asked her to sit herself.

"Please, sit down, ladies. How may I help you? Have you come to see my husband, Simon Maxwell?"

"Oh, no ma'am, we've come to see you, for we've been told that you'll be sending your possessions by porter to Panama City, and we wished to make your acquaintance before we leave. I'm Alice Schmidt and this is my friend Glorina Mac-

Gregor. She's the mother of my friend, Polly Stewart, who's indisposed today and couldn't join us. She's so sorry, for she wished to see you, too. But, a slight illness of the stomach, don't you see?"

Susannah got the idea that she meant that the younger Polly was with child, but she didn't say, for the children were listening closely. There were only two chairs, so she offered them to her visitors and perched on the side of the bed in an awkward fashion. It raised her skirts a little, and she hoped her special shoes were not exposed to the sight of the ladies.

"Would you like for me to order tea? I find a cup of hot tea to be refreshing this time of day, do you not? It would take only a moment. They're very helpful in the kitchen."

"Oh, no," said Alice Schmidt. "We can only stay a minute, for we have a coach and horses waiting below. My husband Howland Schmidt told me how very kind your husband is to help us get to California and start his business, that I felt I just had to come and meet you. This is my son, Richard, and my daughter, Samantha, whom we call Sammie, to her disgust. She's such a feminine creature, that the name Sammie seems inappropriate, but she's been called that since her birth, and I refuse to stop. My friend Polly has one child, a boy of six, named Thomas. And Glo has nine children, all grown and with their own families. She's traveling with Polly and Mark Stewart to California to see the ocean. You've always wanted to see the Pacific Ocean, haven't you, Glo?"

Susannah turned to look at the older woman for confirmation of this bold statement, and Glo nodded her head and burst out with enthusiasm. "Oh, yes, ma'am, I've wanted to see the great ocean since I was a child and never thought that it would happen. My oldest brother went west many years ago and wrote of the mountains and the large trees and the whales in the ocean, but, alas, he never came back. We received a letter about Christmas time and never heard from him again. My mother was so sad to lose her oldest son to the wilds of the west. But, my mother's dead, and can't know that her daughter and grandchildren are going to see the ocean." This was said with such determination that Susannah was enthralled with the woman's temperament. She had seemed so timid and shy when they first entered the room. The boy, Richard, began to pull his sister's hair ribbons.

"Oh, my, we must go. The cabby's waiting, and we only came to make your acquaintance. We'll see one another on the steamship, then again in California, I'm sure, and can visit whenever we wish." She rose, marched to the door and opened it. With a gesture for the children and Glorina MacGregor to go before her, she turned at the door. "It'll be ever so nice to have women friends to travel with to that distant shore, don't you think so? I think sometimes I'll go insane with the children complaining and crying, that I just look forward to talking to another woman. Thank you for your kind hospitality. Good day." And, she was gone with a rustle of her silk skirts.

Susannah sat on the edge of the bed for some time, overwhelmed with the personalities of her visitors. Both seemed friendly and happy to be going on the trip to California. Her mother had told her it was her duty to follow her husband wherever he led her. These two women didn't seem to see it as a duty, but as an adventure. She could see that she had fallen into a depression of sorts, but she must do better. She had promised Simon she would go with him to the end of the earth, and she must change her outlook, or he would think her a hindrance to his plans to explore the west. She rose and opened her trunk to see what she would need in the way of clothing, for tomorrow she was going shopping. She would not spend another day in this hotel room, feeling self-pity and gloomy thoughts. She wanted to see the Pacific Ocean and the sailing ships, even if she would ride one across the ocean to reach that mystical land. Susannah Maxwell laughed out loud and grabbed her stomach, and realized she was hungry.

*****

When Simon came home from his business dealings with Schmidt and Townsend, he found Susannah in an entirely different mood from the day before. She told him of the visit of the two ladies and the children. She was brimming with talk of oceans and sailing ships and silk skirts. He wasn't sure what one had to do with the others, but as long as she was happy, it was well with him, also. She laughed when she told him of Glorina MacGregor, mother of nine children, but determined to cross the oceans to get to California. He was pleased that his plan to find some women companions for her seemed to be working, for he was certain that Schmidt had sent them to her.

In the days that followed, plans were made, contracts signed, animals trained and wagons checked for flaws or cracks to be mended. There was a great deal of plans to organize their belongings and packed goods, which had to be sorted to different porters, and the chore of loading Schmidt's wooden crates, for the items were bulky and heavy. The three ladies, either together or separately, explored the stores and restaurants available, although much of the city was still under construction and inaccessible. Polly Stewart joined them when she felt well, with her son, Thomas. It became quite common to see the ladies and children in the lobby discussing the day's plans or returning from a shopping trip and sorting out the various packages, for the one room was too small for such a contingent of people. Susannah also went to their hotel for a visit between the ladies. They took the children to the parks on good days and taught the children games or their letters.

What a magnificent sight, Simon thought one day, as he walked by the park and saw the ladies sitting on the grass, their skirts billowing out beside them, watching the children at play. His heart jumped into his throat with the pride he felt for his woman, his Susannah. He must write to his mother and aunt and tell them about the scene. He must write to Ezekiel Clark of his daughter's renewed enthusiasm toward the trip since she'd met the other ladies on the trip. He would be gratified to know that Susannah was happy in her new life.

On the appointed day, the porters lined up along the Camino Real, the road to the barges and the paddlewheel steamers. There were perhaps a hundred men to transport all their supplies and materials for the trip to Panama City. Simon and the other men had been assured that the barge drivers were experienced and well able to see that each passenger crossed safely along with their goods. Even so, it was a perilous time. They had to hire a second barge, in addition to the one Simon purchased. The mules and drivers were allowed on one barge. James Townsend knew the six mules well, for he had chosen them himself. He led off with confidence. Behind him came the mules of Schmidt and his family. They would soon board paddlewheel steamers together, and from there, make their way to Panama City. Simon and Susannah wished the caravan the best of luck, for they wouldn't be boarding the barges; and they departed atop their own mules, down the Royal Road, one sweltering step at a time, to their departure point on their more luxurious mode of transport.

****

The time spent on the paddlewheel steamer was the most pleasant part of the journey across Panama. With Simon's hired help, their luggage was transferred from the barges to the steamer while Simon and Susannah sipped tea under a shaded veranda attached to a shore-side building. They awoke each morning to the slap-slap of the wheel on the water, and the chugging of the steam engine became a background noise drowning out the jungle sounds surrounding them. Meals were served on white linen for the first-class passengers, and on long boards resting on trestle legs for the masses. The barge with the mules followed alongside, and new mules were hired at Cruces for the fifty miles to Panama City. There, Simon, Susannah, Townsend, and Schmidt and his family took four nights in a hotel before their ship departed for California. The city was well-established. It was small by New York or Boston standards, but it had all the rudimentary requirements for civilized living, and their time there was pleasant and relaxing. It gave an opportunity for Townsend and Schmidt to oversee loading their supplies, and for them to sell their mules, for they wouldn't be traveling to California with them. The barge Simon had purchased remained in Cruces, and although there was no buyer yet, still it seemed to him to have been a good investment.

— 26 —

The weeks seemed to fly as the *Scottish Clipper* moved slowly through the open seas of the Pacific. Once a mighty whale rose as if from the depths of the earth and plunged with a great splash back into the water. A lookout announced that the Baja Peninsula was in sight, across the Cortez Sea. One of the passengers remarked with sarcasm that it was called by some the Gulf of California, but neither Simon nor Susannah disputed the name of the land strip. For a time, Susannah thought they might sail into the Sea, and as she didn't know the route to San Francisco, she supposed there was a way through that she didn't remember from her recent lessons with maps. After many hours, however, the ship banked to the left, the sails shifted position with men scampering up and down the masts to adjust them, and the *Clipper* aimed securely out to sea again.

In San Francisco, Simon found a hotel for himself and his wife, and accommodations of a lesser nature for those who traveled with him. The city teemed with men gathered to chase their elusive dreams of gold and the riches they would bring: Russian sailors in vivid colors banded by contrasting fabrics and striped shirts, with jaunty white caps; Canadian fur trappers in buckskin and high-topped, beaded moccasins; and Bavarian sheepherders in their tall stockings and suspenders, with jaunty feathers in their caps. Chinese workers rolled barrels along the wharves, revealing long, braided queues and wearing stained, blousy white garments, tightly fitted around the ankles over pointed shoes of felt or leather.

The streets were made to feel safe by the presence of Army and Navy uniforms, of the U.S., Mexican and French varieties. The American sailors were easy to identify with their full shirts with wide lapels, loose trousers, and sashes with ends swinging free. The occasional Chinook Indian walked the streets with the assurance and stance of someone whose opportunities were now boundless, if he didn't give an inch to the white interlopers.

The Middle-Eastern Arabs and Jews working alongside in the city, from open-storefront venues to markets along the wharves, seemed to be unaware of the differences in their religions, and instead finding profit to be their connection to this new life in the burgeoning city.

The most predominant of the city's roughly dressed and often coarsely behaved inhabitants were those in transition from the decks of ships with their tall masts filling the harbor to the gold fields further east and north. The presence of women was sparser than that of men, many being of an unsavory variety and working out of the saloons that seemed to be everywhere. Occasionally, a well-dressed female in a low-cut gown exited an enclosed carriage to enter a shop, only to disappear back into her carriage's safety when her shopping was done.

Simon roamed the streets, sometimes accompanied by Schmidt or one of the other men, gazing in wonder at the rude shacks, built from the wood of the ships broken apart in the harbor, leaving them as bare bones from a large animal. There were tents fashioned of gray or dingy sails stolen from the mainsails of the whalers and clipper ships. Along the crooked streets were flat board sidewalks between the structures to protect pedestrians from the mud and manure of the alleys and byways.

On the second day of July, Polly Stewart gave birth to another boy, and they named him Malachi. The blacksmith beamed with pride. Polly made a quick recovery and soon joined the other ladies as they walked along the streets. Her mother, Glorina, had spent time knitting caps and booties, but it was much too hot in the city for such items. Alice loaned her some cooler cotton overgrown clothes of Richard's that she had saved.

It was a sad but strangely gratifying farewell for the group who had traveled from Panama together. Mark and Polly Stewart, their sons, Thomas and Malachi, and her mother, Glorina MacGregor, found a hotel near the bay, where Glo could see the ocean that she had dreamed about during her long life. They promised to write whenever an opportunity presented itself, but with no permanent addresses for any of the groups, the idea was met with some doubt that a letter would reach them.

James Townsend proved to be a wonderful storyteller. Susannah decided to write his stories in her journal. She conveyed some of the humorous ones in her letters to her siblings, not knowing if they would ever read them, although she was always careful to ask Townsend's permission. He grinned at her and said he would think it an honor if it pleased her.

Townsend wanted open farm land with a few trees to build his house and barns and provide shelter for the animals. Simon sold him one of his horses for a token fee, to save his pride. He and Simon formally shook hands with a deep respect and admiration for each other. Susannah gave him a hug and a kiss on the cheek, to his embarrassment. She'd grown to love the storyteller as though he were her older brother. In many ways, they had grown closer than her dear brother, Anthony. He traveled alone to the south with his saved wages in his pocket, his self-esteem fully restored. Riding his new horse, Townsend looked back and waved a last goodbye. Susannah wiped the tears from her eyes, as she watched him go.

*****

During their sojourn in the town, Susannah wrote a long letter to her sister Mary explaining all that had happened since she had seen them in Boston. She prepared letters for her father and her mother, with a special note to her brother, Anthony, about the noise and clatter of hammers and the scream of saws as the people built their crude shacks. She sent a small package containing odd shaped leaves, small multi-colored stones and a hawk's feather she had collected on her trip through the wilds of Panama for her younger siblings.

She also wrote a polite letter to Simon's mother thanking her for her kind hospitality while she stayed in her home. It was the second letter she wrote to her, the first being sent from Panama City, this time including some of the more frivolous and entertaining happenings aboard the ship. Susannah had been brought up to regard her social duties as very relevant to her relationship with her husband, although she hadn't enjoyed her stay in the Maxwell home.

Simon spent about two weeks finding wagons to transport their baggage and personal effects, as well as the milling and lumbering equipment they'd brought with them. With the run on the gold fields, prices were astronomically high, and he had to resort to threats of legal action in several cases to convince shopkeepers to sell to him at prices that were merely extravagant rather than crushingly exorbitant. Soon they were ready, and the group of wagons left the bustling city and crossed the California grassland. The women and children walked as much as possible to relieve the mules of their weight. Without a word of explanation to the other members of their party, Simon made sure that Susannah didn't strain her ankle and foot. He would come by and casually ask if she would like to ride behind him on his horse, or carry her to the wagon and place her on the seat beside Paget Shaunecy when he suspected she was in pain.

The wagons rolled into Sacramento on a perfect cloudless day, where they settled into a hotel until Simon and his business partner could file their land claims. A few weeks later, they followed the coastline until it disappeared in the rugged tree line of the northern lands of the western coast.

Simon, Susannah and the Schmidt family were heading to the land of the Big Timber. Both Simon and Schmidt chose land adjacent to each other and parallel to two great flowing rivers, fed by the snow melt of the high mountains. There were other smaller streams in the water basin. To Simon's surprise, there was a small settlement named Twin Rivers perched beside a rugged canyon fashioned by a raging stream. With a little persuasion, the Shaunecy brothers agreed to remain and work for Schmidt at the sawmill. Mick Shaunecy laughingly proclaimed that maybe there would prove to be gold on the site.

Schmidt chose land on the banks of the river, for the power needed to run his large log saw. His home would be about one hundred yards further uphill from the river. About five miles away, Simon Maxwell chose a more imposing site and decided to build his cabin high on a ridge, where Susannah could see on clear days into the valley floor and the high, snow-covered mountains in the distance, once the trees were cleared away from the ridge.

As he had promised in the contract signed by the two men, Schmidt hitched the mules to the wagon and went deep into the forest for dead or fallen trees to begin building Simon's cabin. He set up a makeshift mill at the river site to split the logs needed for a temporary home. While Simon and Howland Schmidt worked on the cabin, the Shaunecy brothers built the shell of a barn. It stood two stories high, with a loft for storage.

The four men worked from dawn to dark. It was already deep into July, and the men didn't know how long the pleasant, warm weather would hold. Within a month, a short-term shelter was built and Susannah was able to leave the wagon and sleep in her own home. The men then moved to the second site, to build a cozy, although impermanent, cabin for the Schmidt family and a small shack for the Shaunecy brothers.

Simon's cabin was built snug and warm. It had one large room and a smaller room, and a huge fireplace. Simon and Susannah slept in the small room and used the larger as a social area and kitchen. He began immediately to make shelters for some chickens and a pig that he bought while in San Francisco. He built a lean to at the back of the cabin, which was used for storage and as a root cellar. Everything was removed from the wagons, so they could be used to haul logs. Paget Shaunecy came home one afternoon with a deer wrapped in a canvas bag, already drawn and quartered. It was a welcome sight for the ladies who hungered for fresh meat.

By the first of September, both families had their own separate cabins, while Simon rode each day the five miles to help Howland Schmidt build the sawmill beside the river. Susannah joined them on the day the large log saw was removed from the wagon and placed in its permanent position on the long table they build for it. The rest of the contents of the Schmidt family wagon was placed in their temporary cabin, and a root cellar was dug.

The women cooked a chicken soup with corn fritters and apple pie. There was hot coffee for the men, and as a special treat, apple cider for the children. Simon planned to return to Sacramento as soon as the weather permitted to buy more farm animals and a milk cow. The day proved to be a birthday celebration for Howland as well. Alice brought out the hidden toys she had purchased for the children in San Francisco. Tears of remembrance filled Susannah's eyes when she felt the loss of her parents and siblings in the large rambling house in Boston. Simon felt compassion for her as he told of his own more formal days as a youth in the big house on the other side of the city, for he was an only child, and had only a few cousins to remember from the days of his childhood.

They sang songs of old times, and Howland said a prayer for peace and prosperity in the valley for them and for all the people who had journeyed together from Manzanillo and Panama City. Simon and Susannah left for their own home shortly before sunset. They spent the evening discussing the day's joys and, with great solemnity, made a toast to each other with apple cider for many more years together as husband and wife, Simon said. He kissed Susannah and went to bed content with his lot in life. Susannah was not so pleased, for she was still not in the family way.

— 27 —

September turned to October, and then to November. When the weather was fine, the men felled logs and sawed them into lumber of different sizes and shingles for the roof. They built a huge shed to house the wood so it wouldn't warp in the inclement weather. The stack increased in size daily. Schmidt drove into Sacramento and placed notices on trees and in the business windows of those merchants who would allow it. WOOD FOR SALE. Underneath were directions on how to reach his place on the river. Simon gave him a draft on his bank in which to buy the supplies and any additional tools or equipment he might need to build a fence and large cabin for his hired hands, which they expected to be able to need soon.

When Schmidt returned to the sawmill, Simon found his partner had brought back letters from Sacramento to the mill, one which was from Townsend saying that he had found a good claim and had several friendly neighbors to help him get started with his farming. He mentioned a certain Louisa Granville, and Susannah wondered if a romance was in the offing for the two people.

Another letter was from Polly Stewart, bubbling with enthusiasm for the rocky cliffs and foaming waves of the Pacific Ocean. She wrote that they had seen some sea lions sunning themselves on the rocks. She reported that her mother had caught a chill walking in the icy cold water and sand, but was on the mend. Thomas was thrilled with the carved horse and wagon that Alice had given him for his birthday. They had read all their books and hoped soon to see a vessel from the east with more supplies. The only habitation around them was a small Spanish fishing village on the coast. They sent their best regards and hoped for a prosperous new year for their friends. She enclosed a mailing address, but it might take weeks to reach them, as they were quite isolated on the farm.

The letter teased Simon with a desire to explore the coast himself and see the ocean waves roll onto the shore. But, he had a responsibility to his wife and an obligation to see that Schmidt's business was a success before he went tramping on any explorations.

There was awaiting them at Sacramento a short and abrupt note from Jacob Maxwell that all was well in the home. The other letter that had followed them from Boston to San Francisco and thence to Sacramento was battered and water-stained, and Schmidt laughed when he told Simon that there was postage due. Ezekiel Clark wrote a more effusive letter which gave out a small tidbit of news about each of his family members, from the oldest to the youngest. He added his opinion of the bribery case that Susannah had been interested in before the Caruthers' ball. Susannah was right. The previous case that she had discovered in the dusty book in his office was a deciding factor in the case. Susannah was gratified that she had been correct in her assumption. She and Simon discussed the merits of the case for several hours.

*****

In mid-March, Simon found the time to plow his fields for the spring corn crop. It was a perfect day. The sky was an azure blue, with only a few white, puffy clouds sailing the open space. The breeze was cool enough to worry the cotton cloth of his blue-plaid shirt, and the new denim waist overalls felt comfortable on his legs.

He had paced off a section of perhaps fifty yards wide and twenty yards long, that he thought he could comfortably plow in one day, not really knowing how the mule would react to the chore. Placing stakes at each corner, he had strung cords between them to use as a guide. Spending time at the sharpening stone to put a sharp edge to the plow had cost him another hour of his time, so when he finally hitched the mule to the plow, the sun was already warm on his back.

Yelling at the mule to move out, he planted his feet squarely behind the plow, with his hands on the handle and prepared to make straight rows to plant his seeds. But, nothing happened. The mule wouldn't budge, and the plow didn't move. He yelled again, louder, but, still the mule wouldn't budge from his place in the green grass. Instead, he tried to drop his head to eat of the verdant grass.

Frustrated, Simon laid the plow on the ground and went to the mule, pulling at his yoke, and whispering soft words of praise. Pleased at his efforts, he returned to the plow, and waited. Suddenly, before he was ready, the mule loped away, dragging the plow, and the man behind him.

"Whoa!" Simon yelled, but he couldn't keep up and had to release the plow. He fell flat on his face in the dirt. The mule ran to a tree and stood, calmly nibbling the grass. Simon was so angry, he started using every curse word he remembered from his university days. He walked to the mule, and with the great strength in his arms, he tugged and pulled the mule back to the starting point. Sweat now ran down his armpits and off his face.

Positioning the mule, the plow and himself in the same place, he yelled at the mule to move. Surprisingly, the animal did, for about two yards and stopped. Simon hauled the plow back into position and yelled at the mule again. This time they made about ten yards before the stubborn mule stopped.

Simon could smell the freshly turned sod, the dampness on his face and the manure the mule had left behind. In frustration, he lifted the plow out of the soft, black soil and unhitched the mule. Leaving the plow in the dirt, he walked the mule to the corral and turned him into the pen, then sat on the ground near the barn. He pulled off a glove and looked at his hand. It was rough and calloused, and the nails were chipped and broken. He pulled off the other glove and angrily threw it on the ground. These were not the clipped and well-manicured hands of a gentleman. A tear fell from his left eye, and then another, and great whimpering sounds came from his mouth.

He looked at the field, its white cords strung between the stakes, the plow laying on its side, and a swarm of birds now pecking at the newly turned earth, searching for seeds or worms. He needed a friend. He picked up his glove, rose and walked to the house.

Susannah was standing near the stove, stirring a pot of

beans. She turned at his entrance.

"Susie, my dear. I should have stayed in Boston. I'm a lawyer, not a farmer. I can't even get a mule to pull a plow." He laughed in frustration.

"What?" She blinked in surprise and put down her oversized spoon.

"The mule, he wouldn't pull the plow." He said it so mournfully that Susannah came and put her arms around her man.

"Oh, Simon. What you need is food. Sit there, and I'll give you some bread and sausage." She walked in her special shoes to the counter and brought back a day-old loaf of bread and placed a plate of sausage in front of him. She poured him a cup of coffee from the pot on the stove. "Now, explain to me, my dear."

And, as Simon began to eat his bread and tell of his frustration, the events of the day seemed to take on a more humorous slant. He gazed into Susannah's sparkling eyes and sighed. He finished his repast and stood, ready to tackle the mule again. She followed him to the corral, and with an encouraging smile and a wave of her handkerchief, he walked the mule to the plow, hitched it and started with new determination.

By the time he was ready to stop for the day he looked back at three long, almost straight rows of turned sod and laughed. The birds had multiplied, were gathered in the dirt, and circled the field in anticipation of the feast that awaited them. He lifted the plow, walked the mule to the barn, unhitched the plow and released the mule into the corral.

As he stood near the barn, Susannah joined him, and he gave her a hug. She smiled. He was pleased with his work for the day. They strode together to the house, up the steps and into the door. Tomorrow he would do better; he knew he would.

By the end of the month, the small field of corn was planted, and the kitchen garden was ready for the vegetable seeds he had brought with him from Boston. They celebrated with a dried-apple pie and clotted cream for their dinner.

During this time, Simon discovered it was proving difficult to postpone returning to his "lawyering" life. He'd traveled across the country to avoid his being trapped in a highly-educated and structured lifestyle, so that he could practice his skill and still have time to live out his dreams of exploring the wilds of this new land; yet his mannerisms and well-thought out consideration in dealing with those around him tagged along after him, not letting him escape so easily.

In addition, Simon felt drawn to the use of his mind rather than that of his back and legs, as he had found farming to be quite tiring. He decided to go into Twin Rivers for supplies.

A wealthy banker whose wife had filed for divorce against him heard of the young lawyer taking up residence on the river, and he accosted him as Simon was in his wagon heading to O'Malley's Mercantile and Feed.

"You, fellow!" A tall, burly man, perhaps pushing forty, and well-dressed in shined shoes that were only a little dusty; brown trousers; a coat of dark wool with narrow stripes; and a top hat so deep brown it was almost black, called to Simon. A silver-colored vest strained its buttons as the man walked.

"Whoa, Barry." Simon pulled his draft animal up, slowing his wagon, and when the conveyance came to a full halt, he clucked at the animal, gathered the reins up, and wrapped them loosely around a wooden peg in the floor of the wagon. "Stay there, Barry. We'll move on in a moment."

Simon turned to the man who'd called to him. He was walking in a stately manner, unhurried, as if his dignity was more important than the business—of whatever sort—with Simon might be. Simon wondered whether the man would have continued to call if he'd simply driven on by. He thought of Schmidt, however, and his circulars and flyers. Perhaps the man had seen him in the wagon, and he figured Simon and Schmidt were connected. He'd be right, if he did, although Simon wasn't Schmidt's employee, neither vice-versa. If Simon, however, could help build Schmidt's business by taking a few moments of his time, that was very neighborly and possibly profitable to Simon, as well.

Simon clambered down and addressed the man, who'd drawn close enough to speak without raised voices. "I trust you don't mind. It took me some distance to slow the horse. I don't believe we've had the opportunity to meet. My name is—"

"Mr. Maxwell. How do you do?" Tall and Dusty held out an arm, extended, but not so far as to make it easy for Simon.

"I am well. You are?" Simon leaned in, grasped the hand and released it after a quick shake. In the feel of the man's skin, and the grip of his muscles, he recognized who he was dealing with, or what, in any case. There were those who shook with a limpid dandiness, because they didn't want to shake at all. They desired, instead, to sit in a comfortable chair and have others do their work for them. Then some gave a firm shake, with warmth and sincerity in every muscle. There were few enough of those, for certain. This man? His touch had been hard and forceful, that of a man who wished to make his presence known to cow weaker minds.

Simon wasn't a weaker mind, and he was focused. His classes to become a lawyer had trained him to pay attention to what he wanted and to go for it with measured skill and icy determination.

"Weldon Forney, prominent man-about-town, and owner of the local bank. You can see it there."

The man pointed, and sure enough, Simon looked down the street and found a red-brick structure of about three stories, with a transom door centering the edifice, high crown molding above the door, and three tall windows on either side, each separated by a double line of bricks. The dusty street was rutted with wagon tracks from the last rain, although repeated traffic had beat many of the high spots down. A shingle hanging out front, in metal, and attached to a filigreed arm of dull brass, said it was the Forney Bank, Inc. The elevation was the full three stories in front, but the roof sloped rather steeply toward the back alley, only allowing space for two stories at the rear. A clothesline was strung from one of the back windows, and Simon decided that Forney must live in the space above the bank. It wouldn't be his choice, but it would provide protection to the bank's customers.

One very unusual thing Simon noticed was two pots of winter pansies outside the front door of the bank. Both looked well-cultivated and healthy. The upstairs, along the sidewall, had windows lined with window boxes. The pansies there seemed wilted and forgotten, as though someone had taken an interest, then fallen prey to other hobbies.

Simon turned to the man. "What can I do for you, Mr. Forney? I already have a bank back East, and I've contracted with Waterford at Sacramento Trust Bank for my financial matters. I suppose you might know the man?" It would be reasonable, for Sacramento was truly a city, but even so, it didn't compare to Boston or New York.

"Flint Waterford, certainly. A good man, if you want old-school security. Won't touch the gold miners. Those of us who do will leave him behind. Gold's the currency of California, now." Forney puffed his chest, as if giving a sales pitch and taking a moment to press his wares toward a new customer.

"Then you understand where I stand. I have no interest in gold, myself. I'm a farmer." Simon smiled and made to exit, now certain he'd been an unfamiliar face and therefore a business prospect for the solid, well-dressed man.

"Now, don't be that way, Mr. Maxwell. I come by my information well-said, and I hear you've training in the law. Is that so?" Forney had his thumbs in his vest pockets, and he rocked back on his heels once before settling his feet in one spot.

"I've no offices in California. I've spent my time on my farm, sir." Simon then considered that he'd brought a set of law books with him. It couldn't hurt to earn a bit of goodwill in this far land. It might be that Forney would someday use him for a reference, and if people thought well of him, it could only be to his benefit. He amended his words. "I'll be glad to listen to what you have to say, if you wish to discuss my training."

"Come with me, Mr. Maxwell. Let me buy you a cup of coffee, and we can discuss this in private."

The "private" he took him to wasn't really all that private, but it was off the street. In a wood-faced building just across the street, they entered an eatery named Bertha's Biscuits and More. Forney grinned and said the "more" was some of the best coffee and desserts in the city. The room had a plank floor of raw wood, although it was clean, and in spots, polished with many footsteps. About twenty tables graced the interior, with clean, white tablecloths on each one. A large, pot-bellied stove took up a sizable portion of the floor right in the center. A counter was on one side, and it partially blocked the view of a large,

187

wood-burning cook stove. A heavy, pretty woman with her hair bound in a pale-blue bonnet called to Forney, telling him she'd have him a cup of coffee as soon as it warmed, and did he want one for his guest.

Forney raised a hand and replied, "When you get it done, Rachel. Might take a piece of apple pie, if you have any."

"Peach do? It's all Bertha had time for, today."

"I do like peach. That and coffee'll be fine."

Rachel went back to her stove, and Forney motioned Simon to a table near the window. Two other tables were occupied, and Simon noted that theirs was near neither. He glanced to take in the pressed-tin ceiling, and the sooty ring near where the stovepipe punched through the ceiling. The stove wasn't heated today, as it wasn't especially cold outside, and Simon thought a cook stove the size of the one behind the counter was surely adequate on all except the coldest days.

Rachel appeared with two cups of coffee, telling the men she'd have the pie right there. Once two slices were delivered, Forney lifted his spoon, cut a bite from his and lifted it to his mouth.

"It's good, Maxwell. I can call you that without offense?" He bit into the pie and smiled for the first time.

"No offense. What can I do for you?" Simon eyed the pie and coffee. Steam swirled from the cup, and it certainly smelled good. He took a sip, all the while watching Forney as he took a second bite of pie.

"The pie's good, Maxwell. Try it." Forney swallowed, and he downed his third bite with a jolt of the dark brew.

It did look good, and Simon cut a piece and placed it in his mouth, surprised at the intense flavor. He would need to bring Susannah to this place, when he next came into town.

"You see, it's like this, Maxwell." Forney rested his fork on his plate, only half the pie eaten, and he placed his arms across the table at his waist and leaned forward. He proceeded to tell Simon about his wife, who, after filing for divorce from him, now expected a large settlement. Forney refused to pay. He didn't mind keeping her in housing and a servant, as he had the funds to do so, but she threatened to take their son and move to Los Angeles, if he didn't pay more.

It turned out that his wife left him, accusing him of neglect and cruelty. It was a great deal of money, as now, two years had passed. He wondered if Simon was interested in pursuing the matter in the courts, if Forney could come up with proof his wife was a wanton woman and had been with other men before their divorce.

Simon saw the truth of the matter: that he'd come to him because he didn't want his business known. If the Sacramento businessmen and private citizens found out he had used under-handed practices to defraud his ex-wife of funds that were right-fully hers, his banking business would suffer. Simon thanked the man for his interest, explained that he had no experience with domestic cases, and that starting his new farm would take up far too much of his time to allow him to pursue such an in-volved case. Forney seemed disappointed but resolute, as if he hadn't really expected Simon's help, but it had been an oppor-tunity too good not to pursue. As he left the restaurant, Simon noticed that Rachel stepped to the table to collect the used plates, and Forney took her hand and held it longer than was proper for a banker stopped by for a coffee and pie.

When Simon returned home, he plowed the kitchen garden and planted the seeds he brought with him from Boston. He plowed Schmidt's garden as well and planted a crop of wheat, thus fulfilling two of the requirements in their contract. He dug trenches for irrigation to his own wheat and oats patches.

He didn't say a word about the banker Forney's offer to him, except to tell Schmidt that he'd met him, and Schmidt might see him when he was in Twin Rivers.

— 28 —

In May, Simon finally found the time to return to Sacramento to buy supplies and hire some men to help them. He left Susannah in the care of Alice and Howland, for he didn't want her to be left alone.

It was while Simon was gone to the city that Alice first discovered Susannah's disability, for she tripped over an unseen stone in the path to the Schmidt garden and couldn't stand without help. With tears of pain on her cheeks, she explained without drawing their pity for her situation. The children had to be told why Aunt Susannah was crying, and Schmidt came from the sawmill to find what caused the upheaval. It was a sober family around the supper table that night as each absorbed, in his or her own way, the strength and courage of their friend.

While in the city Simon spread the word about the sawmill in the shops and in the saloons. First, one customer, then two appeared. He hired two newly arrived immigrants from the east to help with the work. They were sent into the forest on his own land to haul logs to the mill. He paid their wages.

He returned with a milk cow, which he left for Alice and the children. He brought more chickens and twelve fruit trees, apple and peach, which the farmer promised would bear fruit in a few years. He brought yards of cloth, cotton, gingham and wool yarn for clothing for the others and heavy gloves for himself and Schmidt. He also brought several newspapers, and he and Susannah read and re-read the articles. It was the first time that Simon began to truly long for the company of men of the law. Some of the news was old, and other parts more recent, as newspapers took some time to make it from the Eastern states. They learned that in July of '50, Millard Fillmore of New York took the office as thirteenth president of the United States, and two months later, by a nearly equal vote, the Texas and New Mexico bills were passed, establishing New Mexico and Utah as organized territories. That same month, the new president signed the fugitive-slave act, preventing slaves from being given jury trials or testifying on their own behalf.

More recent papers told of Cuba, encouraging people not to participate in expeditions against the island nation because of U.S. neutrality laws, as well as the new and popular song *Swanee River* and the book *Moby Dick,* published in its first American edition. The news was quite exciting, and they discussed it several times, talking of how they missed the high-spirited stimulation of current events. They discussed their options and decided they would remain one more year on the farm, helping Schmidt and the Shaunecy brothers at the sawmill and farms.

Satisfied that Schmidt had the situation well in hand, and with four men to help with the work, Simon spent more time on his own property. He explored the river to the high cliffs overlooking the ocean and spent the night in the forest, with only the stars and a wool blanket to cover him. Taking time to build a fish pen, he returned the next day to find three large salmon had become trapped from the swift-flowing water. Building fallen cottonwood branches into a teepee shape, he used a flint and matchlock to start a fire and roasted two of them on a stick over the flames. Afterwards, he shot a deer near a clearing he discovered in the deep woods. It ran for nearly a mile before falling, but he tracked the blood on the undergrowth and grasses and found it with no problem. He broke its neck to take the last of the life from it. Hauling it over the back of his horse, he cleaned and cut the carcass into equal parts leaving the skin, horns and hoofs for his own use. He took half the meat to Alice Schmidt for her family. At night when he was home, he built crude furniture from the lumber that Howland provided. First, a table, and then, a bed. It was wonderful, Susannah exclaimed, to sleep on a real bed again.

Throughout May and June, the sounds of sawing wood could be heard in the distance as Howland and Simon, with the help of the hired men, Dawson and Marden, felled trees and made more lumber and cedar shingles. The vegetables were brought in from the two gardens, and Susannah and Alice canned and preserved them for the winter. The children grew in stature, and little Richard helped his papa when he could but was strictly forbidden going to the sawmill.

July saw a large trickle of immigrants who came by ship around the horn of South America. They bought lumber for their cabins and small limbs and branches of raw wood for their cooking fires. Simon hired another man, called Marcus Stansbury to help with his own farm work. With Schmidt's help, Simon grew adapt at judging the price of lumber by the yard and worked less in the forest and more in a makeshift office set aside for his use as accountant and payroll manager. He often went into Twin Rivers for supplies. He had a few occasions to meet with Forney at the bank, but kept his personal affairs private.

Now, there were more men to fell the logs and haul them to the mill, and one man to tend the Schmidt garden and help with cutting the shingles. He proved to be the best worker of all, for he was a skilled carpenter. He went by the name of Joseph Parlander. He built a large shelter for his own use with the help of Simon and Paget Shaunecy. He slept in the back of the enclosure and used the front as his shed to fashion tables, chairs and beds for the Maxwell and Schmidt households.

Throughout August and September, when the garden vegetables were harvested, Parlander and Shaunecy built a larger cabin with a shingled roof for the hired men. With the exception of the Shaunecy brothers, they had been sleeping in tents as their protection from the elements.

It was a good thing, for Simon came back from a trip to Twin Rivers city in late September with two horses, a stallion and a mare, to be used for breeding stock. He brought a goat with two kids to trim the vines and foliage around the area and to provide milk for the people.

Simon and Susannah celebrated their first wedding anniversary at the Schmidt place with the family and the hired hands. They rode home in silence and wondered at the difference in their lives in one year. No longer a society couple in Boston, Simon was a man of nature who had explored the wild California coast, as he had dreamed of in the days of his youth spent with Benjamin Claret in the wild country. Susannah was a mature homemaker and friend to Alice Schmidt and her

194

children. Her cooking and sewing skills were enhanced by her intelligence and wit. She and Simon challenged each other physically and mentally as they worked as partners and lovers. Their only regret was that no child was yet born of the union. They sat that night and talked of the days in the big house in Boston, of Anthony and her sisters, and her sisters' husbands.

"Susie, we've built a life on this farm, but something's missing. Do you feel it too?" He looked at his wife with a sad longing in his eyes.

"What do you mean?"

He laughed. "I thought I hated the confines of a law office lifestyle and the stuffy courtrooms of Boston, but I find my mind drifting back to the stimulation of my university studies, to the days of good conversation with Anthony and the other students. I'm growing numb, here with the hard work. Would you mind so much if we moved to the city?"

"To San Francisco? Could you build your law practice in that city?"

"No, I'm thinking of moving to Sacramento, to the capital. I saw a copy of the Sacramento *Union* newspaper, and it seemed to be tempting me. Schmidt is doing well, and there are men to help him with the work. I could sell the coastal forest land to him, on terms he could afford, and find a new home in the city. Would you object?"

Susannah gave him a loving glance and replied, "When do we leave? You should be doing what you were trained to do, and I'll support you wherever you choose to hang your shingle." They both laughed, and began to make plans. But, they told no one about their desire to move to Sacramento.

When Schmidt's one-year contract with Simon expired, he was making a small profit and providing for his family. The men made a new compact with only a handshake for five years in which time their separate deeds to the land should be free and clear, having fulfilled all requirements by the government. Simon would continue to pay the expenses and wages of the hired hands, until such time as they both agreed that Schmidt was independent enough to settle all debts and obligations.

In the last week of October, another wagon train arrived in Sacramento to file claims for land. There were no letters from the east for the Maxwell cabin. Alice received a letter from her sister. Two experienced timber men arrived on the train. They individually saw the notices put up by Simon and Schmidt of lumber for sale, and rode to the river to see for themselves.

One man, Caleb Jones, was from Massachusetts, and had a wife, Maggie, and a ten-year-old daughter named Jennifer. Caleb helped at the sawmill and stacked the lumber in the shed. Simon recommended that Jones file his own claim to some land, for his daughter's future. Within a week, a new cabin stood on his land, which was adjacent to the Schmidt place. The supplies that they had brought with them on the train were moved into the cabin, and the wagon used for hauling more timber from the forest. Simon took his mules to the Jones place and plowed a garden spot to fulfill the terms of the requirements that a crop be planted each year for five years.

The other man, a giant in stature, well over six feet, was from Minnesota. His name was Jonathan Terrell, but he was soon called Tiny. On his first day at the Schmidt sawmill, Tiny set off for the forest. It was through his expertise that a form of preservation was established in the wooded area. First, they cut down only one out of five trees in the virgin forest. They used fallen or dead wood only for fireplaces and cook stoves. Next, they built roads through the farms of both Schmidt and Maxwell, so the land could be best utilized without trampling through unnecessary places. Lastly, first one man's land was used for six months, then the other, so neither was being robbed of his portion of the profit for the timber. Simon thought the ideas sound and agreed to the plan. Schmidt wasn't so sure, for he'd worked in timber most of his adulthood, and no one had done it that way before. But, he was wise enough to know that if every log was rolled onto the saw, the forest would be stripped bare and damage the water shed. He agreed to the plan. When Caleb was told of the plan, he decided to let them use his own trees for lumber, earning a percentage of the profit from the sale of his timber.

Another large area around Simon's place on the ridge was cleared, and he plowed and planted crops for the last time. Also, he planted twenty-four fruit seedling trees, sent by his father in Boston on a freighter headed to Vancouver in Canada. It took almost a year for them to arrive, so Jacob Maxwell must have sent them shortly after his marriage, before he and Susannah even arrived at Panama City on their water-borne adventure.

A man was hired by Jacob to care for the seedlings and stay in California, if his son had a use for him. He proved to be a jolly, average sized, middle-aged man, who went by the name of Tinker Calhoun. No one dared ask how he got the name Tinker. He was married to Patience and had two grown daughters, Katherine, called Kate, aged nineteen, who had light brown hair and green eyes, and Loretta, aged one and twenty, who was the image of Emily Caruthers, blonde, almost yellow hair and big blue eyes and long dark lashes. Susannah stood in awe when she first saw Loretta, for she was truly the most beautiful girl she'd ever seen.

Jacob Maxwell sent instructions by letter to his son that if the trees arrived safely, Simon should pay large dowries for the girls, if they found husbands for themselves in California. The two girls were soon being courted by at least a dozen men, both those who worked at the sawmill and merchants from the town of Twin Rivers. The sale of lumber increased dramatically. The growth of the burgeoning city just a few miles away was advantageous, although Simon had a discussion with Schmidt, and they agreed that a booming export business was unlikely. Shipping and overland transportation to other municipalities without railroads or other convenient methods of moving the lumber would never be feasible. One day, perhaps, the forests to the east of Sacramento might make someone a good living, but for now, they were content that their coastal lands were sufficient for their needs. They began to think about replanting the trees they had harvested, for one day, the forest would be gone, otherwise. Terrell offered to commit time to seeing that seedlings were replanted when enough open space presented itself.

Since Tinker Calhoun was hired by his father to care for the fruit trees, the family moved to the Maxwell farm. A temporary shelter was built for them until Joseph Parlander, the carpenter, could build them a larger cabin. It was the first hireling that Simon had charge of, and he thought carefully how to utilize his talents. He interviewed Calhoun to discover his talents and found that he was a cobbler by trade, but had worked at many jobs, including farm work and factory. Simon looked at him closely to see if he was joking. But, the man had no guile in him.

Simon called out the back door for Susannah to join him in the room. She was outside hanging up the clothes she had washed. Susannah almost trotted into the house, so alarmed by Simon calling to her. She stopped on the threshold and noticed that nothing was amiss in the room, only Tinker Calhoun sitting in the new chair Parlander had made for them.

Calhoun popped up from the chair when Susannah arrived, and Simon told her to please sit down. Now, Susannah was really alarmed. What could be so serious that he must call her from her chores?

"My dear, you'll be surprised to learn that Mr. Calhoun is a cobbler by trade." Susannah eyes almost jumped from her head. She looked at Simon, then at Calhoun as though she had seen a ghost. She went white, then red. Simon went to her, thinking he had upset her with his abrupt beginning of the conversation. But, she soon regained her usual calm composure and waved him back to his seat.

"A cobbler? Really, Simon? You can't be serious." She looked at Calhoun as though he were a new form of puzzle she must solve. Then, she burst out laughing. "Darling, your father has surprised me once again with his wisdom and humor. He has been too long under my father's influence, no doubt. It must have been Father who has set this ball into motion. Oh, Simon, how Anthony must be laughing." And, Simon laughed with her at the thought of his old friend putting his head together with Jacob Maxwell, for he was frightened of him the last time he saw them in Boston.

During this exchange between husband and wife, Tinker Calhoun's eyes went from one to the other in quick succession. A frown appeared on his face, for he'd only spoken to Jacob Maxwell at his mercantile store and knew nothing of the other people's names.

Simon quickly sobered, for he wouldn't wish to upset his new employee for anything.

"You said, Mr. Calhoun, that you had worked in a factory.

That wouldn't have been the Codwollader Munitions Factory just outside Boston, would it?" Simon sat almost on the edge of his seat waiting for the answer.

"Yes, sir. Worked for them for four years. Always wondered who this Codwollader might be."

"Well, sir, you're looking at him, or else, a descendant of the old man. He was my grandfather, and I have a few cousins from my maternal side. My mother is his daughter."

Susannah eyes opened wide.

"Oh, Simon," She exclaimed. "I knew you had received your inheritance from your grandfather, but never knew his name."

Simon grinned and turned to Calhoun.

"I apologize for our rude reception to your trade, but it seems that my wife's father and my own have played a trick on us. You see, sir, my wife needs a certain type of special shoe every few years when the old pair wears out. I tried to find a cobbler among the immigrants coming west on the trains this year but have been unsuccessful, and here you were already on your way to our home." This was also a surprise to Susannah and explained his trip to the city the last time.

"A certain type of shoe, you say? What kind would that be? I've worked with several kinds of leather: cowhide, snake, lamb, and deer."

Simon turned to Susannah with a question in his eyes. He wouldn't embarrass her, if she didn't wish the man to see her ankle and foot. "My dear?"

"Oh, Simon, don't be shy. I've seen many cobblers in my day." And, she raised her skirts just enough so Calhoun could see the shoes she wore. The left shoe heel was built of wood and the leather was nailed into it with precision. She turned her foot to and fro so he could see the craftsmanship.

"May I?" And, without waiting for an answer, Calhoun knelt at her feet and took the shoe into his hands. He turned it this way and that, side to side, and stood up. "I can work with you on the shoe, sir, ma'am. It would take some amount of measurements, and I would need my tools, but it can be done."

"Where are your tools?"

"In my bags, sir."

"Do you need a special kind of leather or wood?"

"I have several kinds in my trunk. I didn't know that I would have a position as cobbler when I arrived. I understood from Mr. Maxwell, your father, that I was to take care of the fruit trees and the garden." Calhoun seemed to have grown a foot in height. Simon could see the pride he felt in his profession, and to stoop to gardener must have been a humiliation he endured in order to support his family.

"I'll require you to do that, too, for as I said, my wife only needs shoes every few years. But, if you can find enough business among the settlers in Twin Rivers, I'll set you up in a shop of your own and provide the hides for your leather, if they can be found in the valley. But, for now, I'm sure you can see that I need help around the farm." Simon rose to his full height and shook hands with Calhoun to let him know that the conversation was over. Calhoun turned and walked from the house.

"What do you think, Susannah, have I made a wise decision, or not?"

"Yes, husband, you've made a very wise decision, for it isn't me alone who needs shoes. Think of the women and children who walked across the country. They have need of new shoes. They didn't carry four pair with them as I did, because my father insisted. Especially, the children who outgrow their

201

shoes so quickly will need the use of a cobbler. Why, Alice said last month that the children's shoes were too tight on their small feet. I think Mr. Calhoun will find a fine trade here in the valley. Now, really, Simon, I must finish my wash." Simon watched as she walked away and felt again the closeness that they shared. If only he could give her a child. That was the only thing he seemed unable to do to make her happy.

— 29 —

Another year passed, and the fruit trees from Boston were growing tall in the fertile California soil and sunshine. In May of 1854, the move was made to Sacramento. The farm was turned over to the new manager, a man from Ohio, named Jefferson Ryland, who would report to Simon in Sacramento by mail every three months on the progress of his work. The contract was signed and witnessed by Howland Schmidt, Mick Shauncey and Joseph Parlander. Jefferson had brought with him his wife, Abby, and children, Tim, Arthur, Sam and Priscilla. They would live in Simon's house and care for the fruit trees and the animals.

It was decided that Calhoun would make the move with them. He and his wife Patience had chosen to go to the larger city where business might be more profitable. He left behind his daughters, Loretta, who married Mick Shauncey, and Kate, who married Jonathan Terrell, about fifteen years her senior, in a double ceremony, as the Calhouns packed their things and readied for the move. Terrell agreed to become accountant and payroll manager for Schmidt's sawmill with a rise in wages.

A wedding party was planned that would both celebrate the marriages, as well as say good-bye to their parents, as they journeyed to their new life in the city. Everyone from miles around was invited, those who worked on the logging operation, as well as those who farmed the local land. In preparation for the ceremony, there was music, dancing, log rolling in the river, and tree-cutting contests to see who could chop down trees the fastest. The large, lusty loggers lined up against the burly farmers and raced with axes raised towards upright trees, topped and stripped of their leaves and branches, and attacked the stumps with gusto and verve. When the first one fell, the man was declared a winner, and another race was started.

Overhead, the sun burned through scattered cotton clouds, as birds twirled in the sky, drawn by the remains of roasted hogs with the steaming entrails tossed into a sandy pit. The rough cotton clothes, homespun shirts, and thickly woven trousers reflected the hard work the men did on a daily basis, while the loud voices, bawdy jokes, and drinks consumed reflected the excellent time they were having. One man, Broady Howard, climbed atop one of the standing logs and proclaimed to much laughter that he would marry either one of the Calhoun girls, if they would have him, for Shauncey and Terrell were wet rats who didn't deserve either. Shauncey and Terrell differed with him and called for him to come down to prove his claims with his fists. When he refused, still balanced on the stumpy tree, the two husbands-to-be picked up axes, took each to a side of the log, and chopped away to the cheers of the crowd. When the log began to crack, and Howard came tumbling down,

Shauncey and Parlander hauled him to the river and tossed him in.

As the sun drew the day to a close, fires were lighted, and logs were rolled into place to create a sort of outdoor cathedral. Candles and lamps were set around. The women brought out quilts and blankets to soften the wood, and the families and the children gathered around. As the men lined up beside the minister, Simon rose before the gathered celebrants, raised his hands, and stood until the crowd quieted. He spoke to them in a strong voice.

"Friends and family, today is a time of celebration, both for the daughters of my good friends, the Calhouns, and for the men they'll marry. After tonight, Mick and Jonathan will be free no longer, and the mill'll be better for it, I'm sure." Scattered laughter came from the waiting audience, and Mick ducked his head in embarrassment. "When we first came this direction, I promised a dowry for the girls when they married, and now it seems I'm being put to the test to see if I'm good to my word. I have two money aprons sewn with pockets large enough to hold all the money you've brought with you tonight. I hope it's a lot, because it takes a lot to set up a new home. I've started the dowry aprons with fifty dollars each." Exclamations of amazement came from the crowd. "Loretta and Kate will have these on as soon as the ceremony is finished. Let's fill their pockets full."

As he sat, scattered clapping started and built until voices were calling for quiet, or the wedding would never take place. The girls were in their best frocks, with their hair woven into coils on their heads, and holding wildflowers in their hands. They shimmered with joy in the flickering light from the candles and surrounding fires. The river burbled in the background, and fireflies flickered in the dark. The scene was magical, and once the marriages were complete, Simon and Susannah helped tie the aprons around the girls' necks. The receiving line started, with each person walking by dropping what they could in the ever-swelling pockets.

It was with a small amount of unhappiness that Simon and Susannah said goodbye to their friends and neighbors, but they looked forward to their new life in Sacramento. There was a large party held in the Schmidt barn, with music and dancing. Susannah, of course, didn't dance, but sat on the sideline with her friend Alice Schmidt, and watched the other couples glide by to the familiar songs of old. There was beef stew, chicken, ham and vegetables, with apple pie and berry cobbler for desert.

The next morning the two wagons pulled out for the city. Simon sat high on the driver's seat, his head still a bit muddled from the alcohol he had shared with his friends and employees the night before, with Susannah beside him in a warm cloak and gingham bonnet on her head. Inside the wagon rode the precious law books, her shoes, and the necessary food supplies for the trip. They brought a few pieces of furniture, the bedstead made by Joseph Parlander and a bureau of equal quality in which he had carved an intricate design of his own imagination. Simon was sure the rest of the items they would need could be procured in the city.

Slightly behind, and driving a wagon with four mules, sat Calhoun and his wife, Patience. It had been a sad goodbye for them, leaving their daughters and sons-in-law behind, but they looked to the future with calm acceptance and hope for a better life. Behind the wagon, attached by chains and wooden tongue, was a cart piled high with leather, with which he planned to repair shoes and boots, and a supply of soft and hard wood to be made into soles.

Simon Maxwell and his entourage pulled into the outskirts of the city in the afternoon and made camp along a small stream. Simon was pleased to see that the orderly rows of tents on the well-laid out but muddy streets he'd seen in San Francisco were sturdier buildings in Sacramento, although he noted with chagrin that the streets were the same. He determined that the river might flood some of the homes and shops one day, as many of them were built near to the water's edge. It was a legal conundrum he might become involved in, if lawsuits were raised against the developers of the properties. Store owners and shopkeepers might have a valid complaint for their ruined wares, if such happened. He would have to search out the precedents in his law books. He left Calhoun with the women and rode into town to find a hotel for them to stay in until he could find an office space and house for his wife. He walked to a small restaurant and bought a newspaper at the counter. He ordered a cup of coffee and a piece of berry pie, and glanced through the advertisements. He circled four items that looked promising as he ate his pie and finished his coffee. He paid the bill and asked the proprietor the way to the first address on his list.

He liked the looks of the first hotel, but decided to try the other one before making a decision. He next went to the house listed for sale or rent. It was a few blocks from the courthouse, which would make it convenient for him; and although it was unfurnished, he liked the design and the kitchen area. It had a hand pump and wide steel sink, a wood-burning cook range, and he was pleased to see that there were no steps for Susannah to climb. Simon commented on water stains on the walls and questioned the agent on whether there had been a flood. In early '50, he said, the river had risen with an excess of rain, but dikes were being installed to prevent the occurrence again. In any case, the agent informed him, the framework was of the best quality, as the wood came from the ships that had once lined the harbor in San Francisco. Wood had become a premium with the phenomenal growth in the area, and an enterprising man had conveyed several wagonloads overland, although he said it wasn't worth the cost to do it on a large-scale basis. However, it meant that this was a sturdy house, and not even a flood, the ground shaking or a torrential downpour would cause it to shift from true, unlike some of the weaker structures others put up and rented for even more. Simon was satisfied, paid a deposit for one month, and told the rental agent that he would wait for his wife's approval before making a final choice. He asked for the site of a furniture store and left with a smile on his face.

His next circled article was located in a line of buildings in the center of town near the courthouse. He stopped at the entrance and looked up and down the street. The buildings were small and looked to be hastily built, but solid. A few were two-storied. The one with the "for rent" sign had a wide glass window, green trim and was freshly painted white. He was impressed. He located the rental agency and inquired about the facilities. There were three rooms, including one large room on the front with a pot-bellied stove for heat; shelves lined one wall, and his eyes opened wide to see them. The next room was smaller and bare; the back room was obviously used as a kitchen; it had a hand pump and sink, and to the side was a water closet and small table with a looking glass on the wall. It was perfect for the office of a gentleman lawyer. He laid down a deposit and asked if it might be purchased instead of taken on as a rental property. The agent looked at Simon with a bold stare but soon agreed that they might come to terms if the customer was pleased with the site. He told Simon the place next door was also vacant, and Simon asked to tour it. He paid a deposit for it and left the center of town, satisfied with his visit. He rode back to the camp and sat with Susannah and the Calhoun's for an hour telling them of his findings in the city.

The next day, the wagons were driven into the center of the city, kicking up dust on the unpaved streets, and pulled up in front of the first hotel that Simon had toured. Susannah and Patience Calhoun agreed that they could be satisfied with their rooms for a few nights, and Simon made arrangements for the wagons to be sheltered at the local livery. With all four people now riding in one wagon, he showed them the house, and Susannah had a glow in her eyes as she went from room to room. Patience pointed out features she liked, and the men discussed practical matters, such as furniture and heating costs.

They next drove to the building near the courthouse. Again, the women were busy making plans for occupancy, but when Simon showed Calhoun the office space next door, he balked and said it wasn't large enough for his cobbler's shop. He preferred a place closer to the edge of town.

Simon found a small building in Sacramento that had been abandoned. He bought it and increased the size three-fold with the help of his friend Parlander and his lumber business. In the back section was the home of Calhoun and his wife, Patience. The front became a cobbler's shop.

With the major decisions made, the four tramped to the furniture store and chose only what was needed to start their new life in the city. Two more nights were spent at the hotel, and then the two couples were settled into their new homes. They helped each other unload the wagons and the cart, and set up Calhoun's cobbler shop. Here, anyone in the valley could buy shoes for a cheap price, with the subsidy of Simon Maxwell.

It was while the house was being furnished and the cobbler's shop outfitted that Calhoun and Simon saw two boys prowling down a damp alleyway. When Simon called to them they began to run away. He ran after them and caught the younger one, a blond-haired boy of about eleven years.

"Stop, boy. I mean you no harm." He clutched at the boy's arm, and saw that the older boy had stopped running and was watching him. Calhoun stood silently beside some trash bins, his eyes darting back and forth.

"Do you have a name?" The boy stared at him with fear in his eyes, and Simon dropped his arm, fully expecting the boy to run away, but the larger one came to them.

"His name's Paul, Mister. I'm Saber. Do you have some food? We haven't eaten in three days." Simon saw that the younger boy was crying, and he felt compassion for them.

"Come to the shop with me. You come, too, Tinker." He started walking, leaving the boys with the choice of following or not, as they pleased. With some hesitation, the boys caught up, and Simon opened the door for them. Inside the shop, Simon looked over the boys for injuries or other illness and decided their gaunt look was indeed due to lack of food. He explained to Calhoun that Susannah would be better suited to feed the boys properly, and they closed the shop and walked the boys to Simon's house.

Susannah was in the large room, stitching on a dress. She looked up when she saw the men and boys enter the room.

"Have you some food prepared, Susannah? The boys are hungry." He led them into the kitchen and told them to sit down. Saber sat on a chair, but Paul squatted on the floor, his eyes roaming over the room with curiosity.

Susannah took some bread and cheese from the larder and started slicing the bread. Simon went into the cooler and brought out a glass jar of milk. Reaching to a shelf for a glass, then another, he poured milk into the glasses. He then placed a bowl of juicy, purple grapes on the table. The older boy's eyes grew as wide and dark as a washing tub.

"Go ahead, boy, eat all you want. Come, Paul, don't you want some bread and milk?" The younger boy rose and approached the table where he started to reach for a grape, but drew back as though it might be a trick. "Have you never seen grapes before, boy?" Simon took one and popped it into his mouth. He rolled his eyes in pleasure.

The older boy, Saber, took a grape and handed it to his brother, and took another for himself and cautiously put it in his mouth. He chewed and swallowed, and said something under his breath to his brother. Simon couldn't distinguish the words; they were strange to him. He took a few more, and soon the bunch was gone.

Susannah brought the sliced bread to the table on a platter and opened a tin of molasses. She spread a bit onto the bread slices and laid them on the platter, without a word. She sliced the cheese, laid it beside the bread and turned away to the stove. She opened the door, threw a couple of small pieces of kindling into the firebox, shut the door with a clang and walked back to the front room to pick up her sewing needle.

The boys began to eat the bread and cheese and drink the milk. Simon didn't speak until they had consumed the food.

"Have you walked far, Saber?" Simon said quietly, when the boy had finished the bread and cheese.

The boy's head came up, and he gazed around him, as though searching for a way to escape. Paul nudged him with his

211

arm and spoke in that strange language.

"He's got to pee, Mister. Can we go, now?"

"Tinker, will you take Paul to the outhouse?" The boy hesitated, but it was clear nature was too strong to resist. They left the house to the small building just outside the back door.

"You can go, Saber, if you'll answer a few questions for me. Where have you been and where are you going? Where are your parents?"

The boy shrugged. "We don't have no parents. Our pa came for the gold diggings, but he drowned in the river, and me and Paul been running ever since. We come from Minnesota last year in a wagon train. Our ma died on the farm, and Pa thought he'd get rich, but he didn't. We found our way to the city, but people don't throw away so much food as we thought."

"I see, and where did you stay after your father died? In the gold camp? What language did you speak with your brother?"

"Mostly, but the men don't like us hanging around so we left. Our folks and me came from Poland on a big ship, but I don't remember it; Paul was born in Minnesota. Can we go, now?"

"Do you want to leave, or would you like to have a job and plenty of food every day? I have a friend who owns a sawmill, and he might find work for you, if you'd like to stay." Simon watched the boy's eyes widen again.

"A real job, with food every day? Why would you give us a job?"

Simon heard the door open and Calhoun came in with the younger boy. Paul ran to his brother and began to speak in sharp, agitated words. He pulled on his brother's sleeve, as though to move him.

Saber looked at Simon and then at Calhoun. "He says we

should go, or you'll call the sheriff, and he'll put us in jail." He spoke to Paul and the boy seemed to calm down. He looked at Simon and pulled on his brother's sleeve again.

"Did you ask him if he wants to work in the sawmill? I give you my solemn vow; no one will call the sheriff if you stay."

Simon and Calhoun listened as the boys seem to be arguing among themselves.

"You and Paul stay here for now, until you make up your mind. We have work to do before dark. Ask my wife for more food, if you decide to leave. She'll give you what you need." He gestured to Calhoun, and they left the house and strolled to the cobbler's shop, where they began closing up for the night.

He glanced up when he sensed the boys come near the open door to the building and hesitate. They stood just outside shuffling their feet until Saber knocked hesitantly and cleared his throat.

"Yes, Saber? Have you chosen to stay?"

"What's your name, Mister?"

"I'm Simon Maxwell, and this is my friend, Tinker Calhoun. He's outfitting this building for his new cobbler's shop, and he has equipment that needs to be stored on the shelves. Would you like to help?" He gestured toward a crate and explained they needed to pull out the smaller items inside and lay them out on the newly-constructed shelving.

Simon went into the front room and, using an iron hook, began to uncrate the cobbler's tools. Without a word spoken, the boys began to help him place the items on a shelf. Simon started to whistle and didn't worry about the order in which the tools found their way onto the shelf. Calhoun could sort them out later.

*****

Susannah cooked breakfast on her new kitchen range and sat with a cup of coffee in her hand, reading the newspaper. The two boys sat at the table, their eyes wide in curiosity, breaking apart pieces of biscuit and stuffing them into their mouths. Cups of milk sat in front of each plate. Saber Wasserman frowned at the taste when he lifted the cup to his mouth, but Paul gulped it down and dug his spoon into the soft yellow eggs. They began to whisper in their own language.

Simon finished eating and sat back in his chair and gazed at his wife.

"If you'll write notes to your parents and sisters, I'll write to my parents and aunt. We'll take them to the post office, tour the town and shop if you need anything; then I have plans to spend the afternoon in my new office. Would you enjoy that?"

Susannah agreed it was a pleasant way to pass the morning, and she got out her paper, pen, and ink, and she began to write.

*****

When the four occupants of the house on Claridge Street returned from their shopping trip, the boys settled into a corner, opening parcels containing new shirts and trousers, undergarments and socks. Saber wore a brown hat atop his head, and Paul sported a cap of blue plaid.

Without knowing quite how it came about; Simon Maxwell became the guardian of two minor boys, and they stayed with him and Susannah until he had time to drive them in the wagon to the sawmill and turn them over to Haywood and Alice Schmidt, where they would work at the sawmill until old enough to decide their own destiny.

— 30 —

It was early spring, and the sun shone brightly on Simon's back as he walked the short distance from his office to the courthouse. He drew in a deep breath and thought of the days of his youth and his friend Anthony Clark. Since coming to Sacramento three years ago, he had spent most of his time as clerk to an elderly attorney named Trevor Wells. An average man in size, with thinning hair on top, a long white beard, and a rather thin face obscured by the beard, he regularly wore a suit jacket and cotton shirts with cuffs that showed under his jacket sleeves. His trousers were normally loose, worn inside top boots with a wide cuff that reached almost to his knee. He walked with a wooden cane like a shepherd's staff. His wife, Geraldine, wore her dark hair pulled back severely from her full face, and she preferred dark-colored silks, no matter the season or weather. She tended to pleats across the bodice, wide collars that draped over her shoulders, and darker blouses with lace trim. She always wore a cameo pin at the throat. Simon seemed to remember her son had died years before, and she still mourned. He sometimes wondered what had happened to him, but that was a closed door he could no longer revisit. Today he would be the lead attorney in a case that had come to the Wells and Maxwell Law Office. As he walked, thoughts of those early days in the city drifted through his head.

It was a proud day, when Simon had stood outside his new office and nailed a sign near the front door: *Simon Maxwell, Attorney at Law*. But, although he and Susannah had spent hours reading the law books to sharpen their memories, no one came to the place seeking solace from their troubles. He'd read an advertisement in the *Sacramento Union* for a law clerk with Trevor Wells, and taken his credentials and his letters of introduction from Boston to speak with the man. He found the building on a broad street, rutted as most of the lanes that traversed the quickly-growing city, but with a wide, wooden sidewalk running the length of the avenue. The buildings were clustered more closely than in other parts of the city, some so close as to be touching, giving barely room for a man to access the alleyways behind, or enter and exit the upstairs through the staircases built onto the outsides of the buildings. Wells had a large sign posted so that his business was easily located by the general populace. The building itself was of wood painted like stone, with large, double windows on the first and second floors, and two doors next to each other, although both seemed to open to the same interior room. The stoop was of gray granite and looked to be new. When Simon stepped through the door, a bell rang, and he looked up to see one on a curved band of metal just above the door.

"May I help you?" A youth not more than twenty stood at a

counter to the side. He was tidily dressed, with a dark suit and hair neatly oiled and combed.

"My name is Simon Maxwell, and I'm here about your ad in the *Union*. I wish to apply for the position of law clerk."

"Yes, well, if you don't mind having a seat, I'll let Mr. Wells know you're here."

The man had motioned to two wooden chairs near to a wooden post that was clustered with potted palms, and Simon made himself comfortable. The room was filled with desks, men working, some going to and from large cabinets with trays of maps and other legal documents. He glanced at his shoes, noticed dust, and rubbed them against the backs of his trouser legs. He could only hope for the best. It wasn't the money; he had plenty of that; he needed to be occupied in something that interested him, something in which he could find success. He knew the law, and while California wasn't destitute of the law-minded and legally-learned, he had the opportunity to make a place for himself, if he could get his name known in the circles of the legal profession in the city.

"Mr. Maxwell, if you please." The youth stood before him, indicating his meeting was ready to begin. He walked with him to a wide door that opened in the back of the large space, to an office paneled in a formal style, with raised panels and shutters blocking the view from the rear-facing windows. An old man, dressed in black with a gray vest, sat behind a large desk. His white hair, thin on the top but full on the sides, was combed back from his face. He wore a white beard, thick but closely cropped.

"Mr. Maxwell, come in. Wells, here. Trevor Wells. Glad to make your acquaintance. Washington tells me you wish to apply for a position with us." The man stood halfway and offered his hand. Simon stepped forward to grasp it, and when he re-leased it, Wells returned to his seat with a release of air from his lungs.

"Yes, sir. I read of your offer for employment in the *Union*, and I would like to apply. I have my credentials prepared." He opened his pouch and began to pull his paperwork out.

"There's time for that later, my boy. First, let's talk. Tell me of your qualifications. You look young to be experienced in law. Have you practiced before?"

The discussion had continued, very amicably, and soon Simon had a desk of his own, and he, too, was wandering to the cabinets of maps and legal documents, working on legal cases, copying transcript and filling his days with satisfying and gainful employment.

After about a month, Wells had called Simon into his office and shared that he'd been watching the young man, and he was certain he had a future, whether in his firm or perhaps on his own. He had a legal case he'd like Simon to handle, if he thought he was ready. If so, he'd set up a meeting for Simon with the plaintiff, so that he could hear the man's complaints and see if he had legal grounds on which to stand. Simon agreed, with excitement in his blood, and he shared his good fortune that night with Susannah over a bottle of wine he purchased on the way home.

The case had concerned a Spanish land grant. Simon's potential client was a Mexican grandee, dressed in a wide-brimmed sombrero, with elaborately worked leggings and a shirt to match. A braided, short jacket covered all except the front of his shirt. His boots were black, polished leather, with silver buckles on the side. He was accompanied by his grandson, in plainer, workers' clothes, although he was clean, and his clothing and accessories were in good repair. The youth wore thick, braided sandals, and his dark hair was pulled to the back of his neck, making a short tail of the thick mass. The boy translated in passable English for his grandfather.

"I have much land." The grandee spoke in short phrases, and the youth repeated his grandfather's words for Simon's clearer understanding. "My grant, it is from my grandfather. My wife, who no longer lives, breathed her last on my land. Now, it has been stolen. Americans have come to steal what is mine, and they say the land is theirs." The old man seemed nearly in tears, although he sat proudly and his shoulders were straight.

"Ask him if he has any paperwork to prove his claims." Simon turned his attention to the young man, then looked at his grandfather for his answer.

He did, and he pulled them from inside his jacket. Simon looked over them, easily seeing the boundary markings, but having to ask the grandson to help him with reading several written passages. Simon pulled numerous maps from cabinets and found that the man's property, while clearly his, overlapped several of the largest gold strikes on record. He knew the likelihood of removing that many gold-hungry miners from property they had settled was slim, as there was little way to police who came and went on the vast tract of land marked out on the old grandee's grant. He agreed that he would discuss the case with Mr. Wells, and he stood and shook the hands of the elderly gentleman and his grandson as they made their way from the office. Simon watched through the window as they climbed into a buggy, black with a fringed top, that appeared to be a very elegant mode of transport that had seen better days.

Wells agreed to take the case, and he set Simon to it. He

suggested Simon begin reading the newspapers for relevant information and investigate the law concerning old land grants, especially as California had only recently been won from Mexico and declared its statehood. They needed to know if any other land grant cases had been decided in the courts, especially those from a defunct ruling government.

Simon got Susannah involved, for which she was pleased and grateful. He gathered the paperwork, made a connection with a Spanish priest named Brother Sebastian Rivas, a stooped man in a dark monk's hassock, his hands twisted with arthritis, and his shoes scuffed. His regular job was to care for the vineyards at the local mission. He brought a few bottles of wine as a gift to Simon and Susannah, and a fat bunch of grapes, although they were small, individually. The cleric's hair was streaked with gray, and he sat across the table from Susannah, translating from Spanish to English, as Susannah wrote his words, stopping occasionally to dip her pen into her vial of ink. The old priest's eyes were watery, and he wiped his eyes continuously with his handkerchief. His face was ruddy from the sun, and his voice droned on and on. From time to time, Susannah blotted the ink and turned to a new page.

In the next room, Simon worked at his own desk, occasionally looking through the door at his wife doing what she'd always dreamed of, working on a court case. Of course, she couldn't enter the courtroom and present a legal defense, but she seemed to be enjoying herself.

Simon's time on the case turned into a good experience, for he gained knowledge and skill under Wells' tutorage. The case for the grandee and his land grant was accepted by the courts, and Simon was to be the one to stand and present the case. He was thrilled, excited, and worried all at the same time, as he felt the man was justified in presenting his case, but he'd not been able to shake his feelings that the excess of interlopers would never be successfully ejected from his land. He would give it his best, though, for Wells expected it of him, and he'd never been one to reject a challenge that could serve him well.

The day of the case arrived, and Simon rose from his bed with anticipation. Today he would be tested and he knew he was ready. He had spent the last evening practicing his opening speech with Susannah. Despite his thoroughly prepared case and excellent presentation, the day didn't bring success. The courts agreed that the land grant was valid, but as the men who now resided there had improved the property, they would be granted squatters' rights as long as they maintained their residence there. As for the gold, it was a resource free for the taking, as were wood for fires, water for drinking, and game for eating. There was no mine established on the property by the grandee, so he could claim no precedent for thievery or loss of income.

Simon felt the court decision was biased on the side of the miners, but it was no more than he'd expected. He wished the grandee and his grandson well and hoped that one day, his land would be under his control once more.

Other than the excitement of Simon's new employment, he and Susannah had spent the first months in their new home buying furnishings, and walking the streets to acquaint themselves with the town. The dust from the streets, and the noise of men racing carts after dark were annoying, but it was no more than any other place in the city, Simon assured Susannah. They must get to know those around them so they could look out for one another. They met their neighbors, and she opened a small bakery in the empty rented room next to his office. She spent endless hours baking pies and pastries for the customers who stopped by for a treat in the afternoon.

— 31 —

One bright morning, Simon came to Susannah as she massaged her malformed leg with a thick cream in preparation for slipping into her specially-constructed shoe. He stood at the door dressed in a black suit with gray trousers, shined boots, a silver-colored vest, and a cane in his hand. His hair was tidied with oil and pressed against his head.

"My dear, you've proved such a help to me with my legal work that I would like to claim a portion of your afternoon." He smiled expectantly, pleased with himself.

"You have an entire office of workers to provide you assistance. I have the bakery to attend to, and I cannot let that go." She looked at him for only a moment before dismissing the notion and pulling her stocking out of a drawer to put it on.

"This is special." Simon moved to sit beside her, and he took her hand. "Anyway, you've hired Annabelle Blackburn, and I've tasted of her sweetbreads. You've taught her well."

"Annabelle is a quick learner." Susannah let her skirt fall, the stocking in her hand, and she twisted it as she looked out the window. "I've enjoyed my shop, and still do, but I would enjoy a day spent indulging my old dream. Perhaps I can put in an extra effort this morning, and Annabelle can manage the shop for the afternoon hours. However," and she hiked her skirt and held the stocking out to Simon, "I will not depend on Annabelle to do the baking, for the wares I sell are my reputation, and I'll take no chances, there."

"Which is no more than I would expect from you." Simon smiled as he slipped her stocking over her foot and up her leg, before reaching for her shoe to help her put it on.

"I can don my own shoe, my husband. You go. I'll be very busy this morning, if I'm to help you this afternoon." She took the shoe from him and, with a kiss on the cheek, waved him out the door.

The afternoon turned sultry, and Susannah sat hunched over her tabletop near an open window, pen in hand. Simon was at the courthouse researching a shipping manifest that had been altered from its port of departure in Charleston to its time of arrival in San Francisco. Seventeen cases of high-quality liquor had disappeared. A lawsuit was filed against the shipping company and the captain of the ship, but they claimed immunity, as there is no law upon the high seas. Had the liquor vanished from the port would be one thing, but such was not the case. Simon needed her to research precedent, as the value was quite substantial, and to win the case would greatly benefit Simon's reputation. On her left were three thick law books, markers peeping out from the pages, which were stacked precariously near the edge of the table. Under her pen, the word squiggles seemed to march across the page as she wrote. About six inches from her right hand the ink bottle stood in a small shaft of light from the window. She lifted the pen, dipped it into the bottle and wrote a few more lines.

She sniffed, and coughed. She smelled smoke. Her head came up, and she looked around; no smoke was seen through the window or in the room, but the smell persisted. She turned in her chair and started to stand. A sharp pain rose in her ankle as she stumbled from the seat too quickly.

She heard running footsteps outside the door, and with painful, lumbering, halting steps, made it across the room and into the narrow passageway and out the front door. There on the left, she could see men gathered on the boardwalk near the three-story furniture factory where workers ran saws and sanding machines using a newly-installed steam engine, making the bedsteads, tables and chairs to sell to the ever-increasing numbers of settlers in the city.

Susannah was horrified, for as she stood, a stream of gray smoke from the top floor of the building grew into a black torrent, and the stench was almost overwhelming. Then flames began to appear, and she suspected the building was lost. She thought of Simon, who was attending a meeting of the attorneys from his case at the courthouse. A vaguely familiar dog stood across the street, his head down and his tail wagging in agitation. He gave a weak bark and ran away.

The milk wagon rumbled down the street, the driver hard-pressed to keep the horse in check, as he reared and stepped to the side away from the acrid smell. Neighbors were emerging from their residences, and a ruckus was in the beginning.

She called to a man walking along. He was turned to see the building spectacle as much as moving ahead, and as he was watching, she thought he might have seen something.

"Sir, what do you know of the furniture mill? Is anyone hurt?"

"Ma'am?" He paused and tilted his hat. His eyes took in the building behind her, and he asked, "Is your husband the lawyer? Maxwell, I believe. I recall him in the courtroom."

"Yes, that's my husband. About the mill? Was it intentional?"

"I don't know, ma'am. Maybe the steam engine. I've heard they can explode if not cast properly. If your husband's home, you and he might prepare. If the wind picks up, every house on this street could be in danger."

She thanked him, withdrew from the door and moved slowly to the kitchen area, the pain no longer causing her trouble, and she picked up a cloth. Drawing water from the pump, she held it over her mouth and nose as she returned to the table.

Should she start to collect the precious law books, the reams of paper? Yes, she decided, better to have them ready, in case the fire spread. She found a half-empty wooden box in the corner and began to pack the books, willy-nilly, into it. She stripped the shelves bare and struggled with the weight, as she moved it aside so she could reach to the last section. With her arms stretched out, she shoved the box as close to the front door as she could manage, then went back for the rest of the books. She stacked them near the door, ready for removal. The smoke didn't seem as strong now, and she was grateful for the respite.

As she paused at the door, she saw the bucket brigade begin to form along the boardwalk, dozens of men and a few women now raised by the alarm of the church bell on the corner. She moved back into the office to finish her task, and outside the window saw a horse run along the street in panic away from the turmoil. She wondered if she should visit Annabelle at the shop and see if things were satisfactory there. As it was farther from the mill, the flames would have to spread quickly before the bakery was in any danger.

As she was bending to lift the last book, Simon appeared at the door, laid his satchel on a chair and ran to her side, taking the book, setting it aside and giving his wife a quick embrace.

"We heard the church bells, and no one knew what it was. Then, we saw the smoke from the courthouse windows, and Noah Fogherty remarked that it appeared near my house. I gathered up my things and came as quickly as I could."

"Thank you. I'm worried about Annabelle. I've no way to contact her—"

"I stopped by and told her to lock up for the afternoon. All over the streets, people want to see the fire. No one else'll be in for sweets and breads until this is over." After seeing that she was safe, he seemed to be caught up in the adrenalin rush of the unexpected and catastrophic event occurring just outside their door. "I see you have my law books ready for a quick getaway. Thank you."

"How will we transport them all?" Susannah looked at the collection of books, much greater than the one they'd brought with them from Boston. How had they collected so many?

"If the fire spreads, Tidwell around the corner has a horse and wagon. I'll speak with him and hire it for the afternoon. He'll be glad to help me load the boxes for a fee."

They stood outside the doorway of their office and watched as the fire grew in intensity, and with a gasp of shock, Susannah saw a man jump from an upper floor window. A scream of alarm escaped from her throat before she could stop it; and Simon drew his arm around her shoulders. The man lay for a moment, writhing in pain, then slowly rose and stumbled away, his leg dragging as he went. Two men broke from the bucket line and helped him to safety.

The dog from earlier was back, sniffing, as if it smelled something interesting. A man called to it, then he gave a sharp whistle, and the dog turned its head and began to trot to him.

"That's Tidwell. I want to speak with him." Simon squeezed Susannah's arms and raised a hand and called, "Hey, Tidwell! Richard! You still have your horse and wagon?"

"That you, Maxwell?" Tidwell peered through the smoky haze filling the street, and looping a cord around the dog's neck, he led it towards Simon and Susannah. "Ole Jimpy here was out this morning, otherwise I wouldn't have known this was going on. The missus is at her mother's in Frisco, and I was in the basement working on the boiler. The missus likes to stay warm in winter. You, you got a ringside seat to the best show in town."

"Yeah. About that horse and wagon," Simon persisted. "All my law books are in the house."

"You thinking this might come your way? Nah." Tidwell shrugged it off, and he pointed skyward. "See the smoke? It's leaning away from us. Anything burns 'twill be that direction. It's those people who gotta worry."

Susannah brought the men glasses of water and the dog a scrap of meat. They pulled up chairs from inside to watch the fire progress. Simon questioned whether he should join the fire brigade, and Tidwell advised against it.

"Too many people don't know what they're doing, and the process falls apart. Drop a bucket, and all that water's wasted. Besides, the street's crowded with people doing what you want to do. Next time'll be your turn. And in a city this size, there'll be a next time, I can assure you."

228

True enough, more people were milling around than were carrying water buckets, as the water seemed to be in limited quantities. Susannah had noticed her own pump producing only a small amount of water as she filled the glasses, and she wondered if there would be a lawsuit against the mill or the city if other buildings burned. For Simon's income, living in Sacramento might be a good investment in his profession, and she would need to keep herself apprised of opportunities that might require his skills as they arose.

The building was almost consumed with flame, and there was a sober mood among the onlookers; they had done all they could; despite the plethora of ready volunteers, there was not enough water; and without enough water, there wasn't enough manpower in all of Sacramento to save it. Simon and Susannah, faces somber, their minds weary, turned away as they watched the crowd begin to disperse. The last of the timbers broke apart and fell in, loudly reverberating, and sending showers of sparks towering into the air. What that morning had been a productive, intact building housing about a dozen carpenters and laymen, now lay smoldering and sad. A few small puddles of water gleamed in the light from the sun. The skeletal framework of the metal saws, sanding lathes, and the massive steam engine, now blackened, were all that remained. A lone man sat near the curb, his head in his arms.

At last, Tidwell and his dog bid them farewell, the couple turned away, and Simon led Susannah into the front room. He lifted his eyebrow at the stack of books and smiled at her ingenuity and thoughtfulness.

"It seems I get to shelve the books. This is an opportunity to rearrange them to a more beneficial order." Simon lifted one and opened the cover. He read for a moment then closed it.

"I'll do it. I'm the one who moved them." Susannah rubbed her leg, wishing she hadn't stood on it so long. "Please check on the bakery to ensure that nothing happened and Annabelle locked up properly."

"After I clean up." Simon grinned. Sure enough, soot streaked his skin, even though the fire hadn't come near their home. He built up the fire in the stove and filled the kettle with water. While the water boiled for the tea, he ran a hand over his face. Feeling dirty and gritty, he manned the pump and filled a bowl half-full of water. He grabbed a clean towel and went to Susannah and helped her wash her face and hands. He returned to the stove, poured the boiling water over the tea grounds in the pretty, flowered tea pot, and left it to steep. He gazed out the window and noticed that the hour was growing late. Several men still stood gazing at the lost building. He sighed and took two cups and two saucers from the shelf. He found the last of the day-old bread and cut a few slices, spread butter and jam on each slice, and put them on a plate and took them to the living room.

"Thank you, Simon. Off to check on Annabelle. I'm fine."

"As you always are, my strong and determined wife." Simon kissed her forehead and vanished through the door.

Susannah sat against the curvature of the chair, her head leaning against the back, her eyes closed. She opened them when she once again felt the presence of her husband near her. She blinked at the slices of bread and the tea. She hadn't noticed that she had skipped a meal, so engrossed had she been in her research in the books. She laughed when Simon set the cup near her hand, and offered the plate of bread and butter for her nourishment.

"Everything was fine?" She sipped the tea and realized it

had grown cold.

"With not a loaf of bread out of place." He grinned, and before long, darkness fell on the quiet street that had known such a frenzy in the brightest hours of the day.

— 32 —

And, still no child came to dwell in the Maxwell home. Letters and notes came and were sent sporadically to the East Coast. Schmidt's sawmill was thriving with each new influx of immigrants. Orders were filled and shipped as far away as San Francisco after the mission became a major port city.

In their third year in the city, Simon received a letter of a visiting businessman who wished to make a call. It was his cousin, George Veighton, on his mother's side. Susannah held out the letter as he arrived from the law offices. She seemed excited to have a dispatch from home, as though she couldn't wait for him to open it, no matter what the contents might reveal. Simon pulled off his hat and set it on a small commode off to the side of the door, and he removed his gloves before taking the letter. Giving Susannah a kiss on the cheek, he smiled at her.

"How has your day been, my dear?" He had yet to glance at

the missive, though he knew she thought it important, or it wouldn't have been the first thing she offered him.

"Simon, you tease me." She let her lip jut out as if irritated. Then her eyes sparkled. "Open it. I recognize the name, although I don't know the person. Your cousin, I believe."

He glanced at it and chuckled. "Veighton? Let me think."

"You know it is. Open it." She tapped her foot in an irritated manner.

He made his way to his desk and withdrew a slender letter opener. Inserting it into the flap, he worked it against the thick paper until it parted completely. The interior held perhaps six sheets, all written in a tight hand that Simon recognized as George's. He unbuttoned his coat, pulled out his chair and sat to read. As he finished each page, he handed it to his wife for her to also access everything his cousin had to say.

It seemed the Codwollader's Munitions Factory was diversifying. With the sudden growth in California, and the influx of miners into the local area, an opportunity had opened for possible success in textiles, specifically sturdy clothing, bedding and tenting. George would be arriving in six weeks, and as Simon was the lawyer in the family, and he was already in Sacramento, would he be so kind as to search out a possible location for the new factory and arrange for a lease. Looms, cutting machines, and a set of one hundred sewing machines were en route via Cape Horn and should be there about the time George arrived. He would have his wife, Clementine, and their children, Beth and Claude, with him. He would also need a house and furnishings, and if possible, a horse and carriage, and staff of at least three to run the house. Simon would have full authority to pull whatever funds necessary from George's bank, and an authorization was enclosed. If Simon faced any problems accessing the necessary funds, George would reimburse him any expenses he was out in setting up his and Clementine's new life. Of course, he would also reimburse Simon for his time at his usual rate, for that was only fair.

When Susannah finished the final page, she looked up and studied her husband before speaking.

"Is this good news, my husband?"

"I should think so, although it may require much of my time. George and I were always a good fit, and I understand him well." When she still hesitated, he knew that wasn't what she had asked. He leaned forward and took her hand. "What, Susannah? Do you have reservations?"

"We don't need the money, and you worked so hard to leave your old life behind. Is it simply following you?"

"Not at all." He gently kissed her hand. "This may, instead, be the very answer for which we've prayed. You do remember that my money came from my mother's side. Codwollader's, specifically. I have no fiduciary interest in the munitions factory back East, but I could, perhaps, take an interest in this new venture for my pay. It also might be my step up to my own law practice. Just think, as representative of Codwollader's, I'll get exposure to all levels of Sacramento government, and my name will become widely known."

And so it was agreed. Susannah warmed to the idea, to have family in the same city, and children, as well, for oh, she missed having children around the house. She traveled around the city with Simon as he visited possible locations for the textile factory. Many buildings were unsuitable, as they had poor access or the ceilings were too low inside to include the machinery that George would be bringing with him. Others were shy of windows, as the workers would need massive expanses of glass to allow the lighting needed to weave, cut and sew the cloth into salable items.

Eventually, on a day that Susannah was unable to be present, a large, post-and-beam structure was found very near the center of town, perfect to hire workers and give them easy access to the premises. Simon surveyed it critically, using his wife's criticisms on previous properties to judge whether it was suitable. The interior was flooded with light, as the roof was lined with glassed-in cupolas, which could be opened in summer to allow airflow and circulation. Deciding Susannah would be pleased, Simon signed a lease for six months, paid with a draft from his cousin's bank, and set out on a house-shopping expedition.

Housing proved more difficult, for Simon knew his cousin and his wife were used to luxury. An ad was placed in the Sacramento paper, advertising for a comfortable home for lease for at least one year, with quarters for servants, and generous bedroom space. When the paper came out, Simon brought one home to show Susannah. She opened it to find he'd also placed a large ad for her bakery. It said, Pies! Cakes! Bread! in large letters just above her name and the address of her business. She was very pleased. A home wasn't found through the newspaper. Rather, Susannah heard through a customer in her bakery that a large set of rooms above Campbell's Wholesale Five and Dime Resale Emporium were soon to be evacuated. The family had invested in shipping, and the flood of January 1850 had devastated their interests when their merchandise stationed at the Embarcadero had washed away downriver. The rooms were supposedly quite well fitted out, and they were willing to sell any furniture a prospective buyer might wish to consider purchasing.

Indeed, up a set of well-built and covered outside stairs, Simon and Susannah were introduced to a refreshing breath of air, for it seemed as if the luxury of Boston had indeed traveled across the country to provincial California. The person Susannah had spoken with was the family's cook, she found out, when they toured the kitchen. The rooms had high ceilings, plentiful wood stoves for heating the spaces, and ornate draperies on the windows. The floors were wooden planks, but luxurious carpets covered all but the outside edges. Matching wallpaper adorned the walls, and the ceilings were painted in a trompe l'oeil fashion, with one room revealing a cloud-filled sky, and another with angels peering from above the cornice boards. The furniture had been shipped from factories in the East, and much of it was quite good. The horsehair and velvet davenports were firm but comfortable, Susannah pronounced. There were four total bedrooms, with separate quarters for the help, though for three occupants, two might have to double up. She agreed that Simon's cousins wouldn't find anything better, but it seemed with the quantity of fine furnishings, that if the fittings and fixtures needed to be purchased, the cost might become exorbitant.

Simon agreed, and he negotiated an agreement that would provide a partial payment in advance for the furnishing, the assumption of the building's lease, and if his cousin didn't wish to retain all the furniture, Simon would see to the sale of the remaining items and deposit the proceeds in the local bank. He would write up a contract and return the next day to officially formalize the agreement. He found a livery in the next street that could house a horse and carriage. Simon asked them to be on the lookout for a carriage that could provide transportation for four, and it must be of good quality. He left his card and a small deposit for their trouble. He left the hiring of the servants up to Susannah, as she had contacts through her bakery. She said she thought the family's cook might be willing to stay, if she could be paid in the interim. She would likely have options for additional servants they could hire before Simon's cousin arrived.

*****

On the day of the Veighton's arrival, Simon and Susannah awoke to thick air and the smell of pending showers. The curtains hung limply at the open windows, and even the horses moving through the street sounded languid and morose. Simon suggested that Susannah wear something durable, and he would carry an umbrella should the sky decide to open and drench them all. He expected it would rain before the day was out, and while he hoped it would wait until the evening, one could never be for certain. When finally dressed, Simon was replete in the dress of a modern-day gentleman of substance, with Susannah decked out in a royal blue frock of velvet and white and carrying a thin covering should the rain begin to fall; her special shoe peeped from the edge of a white petticoat bordered by darkest navy.

Simon left the house to retrieve the carriage he'd hired for the day, and pulling it to the door, he made his way inside to let his wife know they were prepared to make their way to the wharf. Overhead, the sky spread like a dome of churning melancholy, and the clouds appeared as towering white temples and gray neurotic pillars; undecided whether to release their water onto the earth or not. As they approached the waterfront, the humidity of the pending weather seemed to suck the life from those already there. Women fanned with small wood and paper boards, and children ran around with hair plastered to their heads. The smells of the waterfront rose thick and rank in the dampness; rotten fish and vegetables, and the scent of hemp and cotton piled high on the wharves came and went with the sullied breeze. A whiff of coffee beans drifted from canvas bags being moved by several sweat-stained workers. A shaft of light broke through the clouds onto the wharf as the people stood lined near the embarkation point, patiently waiting for the ship to dock.

"Look, Simon, I can see the big ship." Susannah grew excited, and she pointed down the river. Sure enough, the steam from the stacks was just visible. Faintly, the sounds of the steam engine carried over the water, a huff-huff sound that was soon drowned by the rising excitement of the crowd. A band had been invited to play, and four men in uniform stood to the side, with a drum, two horns, and a handheld pianoforte. Once the crowd's excitement began to grow, the instruments started a lively tune, and the sounds of the ship vanished beneath the excitement on the wharf.

"It will be good to greet ole George." Simon chuckled, and he lifted Susannah's hand and gave it a quick peck.

As the prow of the ship underneath the towering stacks came into view, she remarked, "All your cousins are on the ship. We'll have real family around again."

"Not all, my dear. Just this one set." Simon smiled, as this was a day of excitement for him, also. He'd worked hard to prepare for his cousin's arrival and wasn't sorry to see a familiar face once more. He took a snowy white handkerchief from his coat and wiped his forehead before slipping it back into his pocket.

At last, the ship docked at the pier, and the people could see the sailors let down the gangway. A stream of people began to trudge down the wooden ladder, and the crowd rushed forward to meet them.

Men in formal attire, casual waist overalls and tall hats mingled with women in fancy hats and wide skirts. Simon stretched to see someone he recognized, but alas, there were too many crowded around the dock.

"Susannah, if you'll move over to that striped awning, I'll see if I can find George and Clementine and come to you there."

"No, my dear; we shouldn't be separated in this crowd. We might not find each other again."

Just at that moment, he heard his name shouted out and looked toward a tall man.

"Simon! Simon Maxwell, is that truly you?" The tall man waved.

"George?" Simon had to look twice. His cousin now sported a full beard, a change from the formerly clean-shaven man.

"So my beard has fooled you. Even my children tell me I should shave it off, but I won't. Since leaving New York, I find there's too much to do and see to shave every day. Ahh! Here's the children."

Veighton was crushed between two youngsters, about five and seven. A very pretty woman joined him, in a pale green traveling dress in a simple cut, with a fringed cloth parasol in a fashionable style. Her hair was up, and she sported small jeweled clips on each ear. She held out her hand to Simon and Susannah.

"Clementine. I don't believe we've met. You must be Susannah. You, Simon, are George's salvation. I hope my husband's requests for help haven't inconvenienced you too greatly."

Susannah, Clementine and the children found the striped awning, as it took some time for Simon to hire a wagon and driver to transport the luggage, the men to settle the crates and cases onto it and to strap it to the wagon. He apologized he had so little space in the carriage, and he suggested the children might like to ride with the luggage, as the wagon would follow them to their new residence, and they wouldn't get lost. He apologized to George, telling him he'd see him at the house.

Slowly, they moved through the streets of the city, dodging a cart vendor at the edge of the street, and Simon pointed out the new fire wagon, red with yellow wheels, and the burned-out shell of the factory. Susannah recounted her memory of the fire that had consumed one full day. Veighton remarked on the fire wagon in the fire house, that surely it would have put out the fire if manned properly. Simon told him with pride that it was at his insistence the city procured the vehicle, but alas, it was purchased after the building had burned.

At the rooms that Simon had leased for them, a servant came down the stairs to help them unload the luggage. Simon led his cousin and their wives inside, with the children pulling at their hands, and they exclaimed their excitement over a fully furnished home. The cook had a meal in preparation, and the odors of the meal reminded everyone that lunch had come and gone, and food had not been served.

Clementine insisted that Simon and Susannah join them for a late lunch, but she was clearly tired, and Simon and Susannah left the Veightons to accustom themselves to their new surroundings, telling George that Simon would call on him in the morning to show him around and take him to view his new

240

factory. His equipment was yet to arrive, but he was confident it wouldn't be long before the factory was operational.

When they returned home, Susannah had stars in her eyes.

"What's this, my love? You seem pleased."

"I am, my husband. It's children, and a woman I can get to know. I informed Clementine of my bakery, and she's an interest in baking. I hope it can be a point of common interest for us to become friends."

Simon assured her his cousin's wife was very pleasant, and he was certain they would get along with all good humor. As they made their way to bed, a cool breeze stirred the curtains, and the couple made good use of their time alone in their home.

*****

Upon George and Clementine Veighton's arrival, Simon and Susannah's life took a livelier turn. There were the children, Beth and Claude, who were likeable and well behaved, and who treasured Susannah's sweets at her bakery. Clementine took Susannah under her wing, and they spent time together both at Susannah's home and Clementine's suite of rooms over the mercantile. On days when the children were occupied with their tutor, Clementine often wore a simple, half-sleeved dress of wool with a plain white collar and joined her cousin in the baking of pies and breads. She shared family recipes from her German background, increasing Susannah's delectable array of sweets and bread for her customers to enjoy.

Simon was called upon to help George get his business up and running. As his cash soon grew thin, he was pleased to take up Simon's offer of a stake in the company in exchange for his business and legal expertise. George agreed that the furniture in their new home was of good quality and suitable, and he transferred funds to send to the family who had lived there previously. The factory equipment had to be unloaded from the ship, installed in the new factory, and a need for workers was posted in the Sacramento paper. Handbills went up over the city, with offers for positions at good wages, and soon all the openings were filled. George contracted with Schmidt to provide firewood for the boilers, as he needed a good supply, and Simon assured him the man had a sawmill, was dependable, and would honor the prices they set. It gave Simon and Susannah the opportunity to travel to the farm, to carry needed materials from the city, and survey the improvements to the buildings, the new roofs, extensive water piping, fencing, and other seemingly miraculous changes Ryland had made. They visited with Saber and Paul Wasserman, and felt they were content working at the sawmill among the rough-hewn men and tall forest surrounding them. Saber had grown into a thin, gangly young man, with the shadowy beginnings of a beard. When asked, he opined that he liked the life at the sawmill just fine, and it was good work that needed doing. They had a fine meal one evening with Alice and Haywood, recounting their times together, and telling what they remembered of their travails in Panama and on the ship from Panama City. It seemed the adventures became more grandiose each time another tale-bearer began a new story.

— 33 —

November 3, 1853
Dear Daughter Susannah,

Boston has become dreary at this time of the year, but I shall not drone on about occurrences over which you can surely have no control or interest. Of more pertinence might be my news to you of our new president and his stand on things political and military. President Franklin Pierce, our new man of power, is strongly in favor of the policy of manifest destiny. He feels certain we shall rule this continent in its entirety from shore to shore, excepting those lands already conscripted by Canada in the north and Mexico in the south. For proof, I offer the Gadsden Purchase and the president's support of Commodore Perry's Japanese venture initiated by Daniel Webster, President Fillmore's Secretary of

State.

Now for my real question, for which you and Simon must put your heads together: There is the problem of what to do about rising tensions and incompatible beliefs concerning the Compromise of 1850, which some had hoped would settle the slavery issue. I don't believe this will be an issue of much consequence in your adopted land of California, but it consumes the conversation at every meal in Boston.

My daughter, I should like to travel to see you, should your mother and I be able to get away. I understand the shipboard accommodations can be quite comfortable, if one chooses the proper vessel. Perchance you will see your mother's face once more. She longs for the feel of your arms again.

In loving warmth,
Your father

Polly Stewart wrote that she had a baby girl, and her mother, Glorina MacGregor, married a fisherman who had a salmon cannery along the northern coast near Monterey. Each year canned smoked salmon found its way to the sawmill of Howland Schmidt for the enjoyment of his employees and for Simon and Susannah.

In the year 1855, after more than four years of marriage, Susannah gave birth to a son. They named him Adam Clark Maxwell. In the fall of 1857, Susannah gave birth to a baby girl. They named her Ann Marie Maxwell, and called her Annie. The following year, at the height of the expansion of the city, she gave birth to another boy named Anthony Jedediah Maxwell, after Susannah's brother and Simon's friend. He was called Tony.

Struggling with his law practice and the responsibilities of a growing family, Simon and Susannah agreed that they would not be returning to the farm. Life in the city had grown to consume their time. Susannah had the bakery, although now with two hired girls, a large, matronly, beak-nosed woman named Tansy Scott and Annabelle to help her in the bakery, and Simon was spending longer and longer hours with his court cases. Taking the time to manage the farm from their city environs was less than practical, and they were receiving little income from it. The cash from the sale would be a boon, and they could consider enlarging the house for their expanding family. Susannah remarked that it was a dream that had come and gone, and she was glad Simon had pursued it, letting it take him across the continent, for they would not be here otherwise, and she had made many friends and a place in the city that was her own.

The sale took some months, as an agent had to be contacted, and the land shown to prospective buyers. A Chinese family, who had prospered in their home country and had sold everything to find a better life in America, offered the best price for the land, and Simon and Susannah were pleased. When Simon came in the house to tell his wife of the pending sale, he found her sitting by the window at the desk he'd set up for her. He stood watching her for a few moments, his love for her swelling inside. The weak sunshine filtered through the window glass and spread across the floor next to the desk, a stack of correspondence in front of her. She took a slender letter opener and slit the seal of a cream parchment, and spread the sheet to its full length. It was an invitation to the governor's palace. She pondered the date for a moment, and set it aside. She took a sheet of clean paper, dipped her pen into the ink pot and wrote a polite rejection. She sighed and picked up the next letter.

"Susie, we have a buyer for the farm." Simon broke his surprise to her. "Jefferson Ryland intends to move to a large ranch near the border with Oregon. All is working out, you see."

"I had no doubt you would be as successful in that as you have been in every area of your life." Susannah set her things aside, stood and gave her husband a warm hug.

When the money rested finally in Simon's bank, they knew that phase of their life was wrapped up, and their lives would no longer be on the land they'd once farmed. They were people of the city, and the law was their life.

*****

When Ezekiel Clark decided to retire from the practice of law after the death of his wife, Julia, the old man caught a ship out of Boston and came to visit his daughter. All his children were now married and settled in their chosen fields of occupation.

On the day of Ezekiel's expected arrival via a steamer from San Francisco, Simon and Susannah stood along the wharf abutting the Sacramento River. The sun was high in a brilliant sky. It hadn't rained in weeks, and the dust from passing carriages curled lazily in the air. The noise of goods being loaded and unloaded echoed against the buildings: the metal hooks and tines, and horses whinnying and neighing. The pumping sound of a steam engine was a vibrato thrumming in the soil. The stack of the steamer was visible first, then the prow, with the word *Star* written in white paint. Numerous people disembarked, from finely dressed matrons, in tall, feathered hats, to immigrants carrying food baskets in their hands. When it seemed there could be no one else aboard, Simon inquired of the captain, only to learn Ezekiel had chosen to wait another day to depart San Francisco, as suitable quarters hadn't been available on the steamer *Star.*

He arrived the next day on the *Princess Anne,* a much larger steamship, along with seventeen steamer trunks, barrels, and other containers, in which they brought a decade's worth of mementos, presents, and other items Mrs. Clark had thought necessary for Susannah to have in California, and had insisted be packed before her death. Clouds began to roll in, darkening the sky, as they loaded his luggage and sundry items aboard the wagons. Rain seemed to threaten, but the sun broke through as they boarded to make their way home.

One morning several days later, as a misting rain was falling, and low clouds had settled over the buildings of the city, Ezekiel, now an old, white-haired man, rose and took a cab to the courthouse. He was stooped and walked with a cane, but his mind was sharp and clear. Inside the courtroom, Simon was participating in the case of a miner named Marlot accused of murdering a man. He was in a brawl at his work site, claiming the man had been a miner with him two years before and had stolen his claim, along with over four ounces of gold. When he returned home, dazed and bleeding, he found his wife with the man, and in his fury, he beat him until he died. He claimed it was no more than horse thieving, to steal another man's wife, and they hanged horse thieves. Simon finished his summation of the case and gazed over the audience. On the bench behind the defendants table sat Ezekiel Clark, gazing in wonderment. Simon smiled.

He turned back to his client and they waited patiently until the jury returned with the verdict. Two hours later, the verdict was read, "Not guilty." Simon drew a breath of relief, shook hands with his client, and watched as the jury left the courtroom. He gathered his papers and stuffed them into his leather satchel. He walked to his father-in-law and put his arm on his shoulder.

"Papa Clark, did you get a thrill like that when you stood in the courtroom and defended a client?" Simon placed his arm around the frail shoulders of the man he had grown to love.

"Yes, but it's better when a man wins." Ezekiel Clark grinned; he refused to believe that the civilization that had grown in the ten years that Simon and Susannah lived in Sacramento was anything compared with the active life of Boston, and he enjoyed teasing his son-in-law about such.

They left the building and strode down the steps; and Simon whistled for a cab. They rode in silence along the street toward home, each man lost in his thoughts. The vehicle stopped in front of the large white house Simon and Susannah had built, and Simon paid the man. He clucked to his horse and drove away. Ezekiel stood as though made of stone, gazing at the tree-lined street.

"Papa Clark, you should come in the house out of the damp air." Simon gazed around, and tried to move the man, but he stood as though transfixed.

"Son, that first day that you came to the house with Anthony, I said to Julia, there's a man who will go far in life. I never thought it would be three thousand miles away from Boston, though. I can see a beauty that I never dreamed possible in the valley and in the mountains behind us. Do you regret that you married my daughter?"

Simon thought a moment, the question rolling around in

his mind. It deserved an honest answer.

"Papa Clark, that day in your library, I thought I would have to stay in Boston and practice the law. I loved your Susie even then, but I didn't realize how totally dependent on her I would become for my well-being. I thought I would explore the West; see the rivers, valleys, the wild animals and the ocean. Be like Lewis and Clark; to be free as the open air and the birds in flight." He paused, and they both looked up as a milk wagon pulled by a brown horse rolled by, splashing water on them.

"Did you do any of that?" The old man's eyes seemed to probe for an answer.

Simon laughed, "I never did see those rivers and valleys except those we saw coming across the Isthmus of Panama, but right here in the city, I have found more happiness than God knows I deserve." He gently moved the man toward the front door of the house, for the dampness wasn't good for him. "Can I tell you a secret, Ezekiel Clark?" He paused on the front porch.

Ezekiel looked at Simon with a puzzle in his eyes. There was a twinkle in his son-in-law's eyes. "What secret, Son?"

"I think I realized that I was content when Tinker Calhoun showed up with those twenty-four fruit trees and told me he was a cobbler. Now, admit it. You and my father didn't trust me to find a way to keep Susie in shoes, did you?" Simon looked across the space to his father-in-law, a grin on his face.

Ezekiel Clark looked like a guilty school boy. Simon thought he even blushed, his face was so red.

"Now, Son, I got to admit it did bother us some. The fact that you were going so far away without us there to see that you did the right thing by my child was certainly in our minds."

Simon laughed, and the sound echoed down the street like the ringing of a bell. Susannah opened the door and welcomed the men into her warm kitchen. She never knew what the joke was about, but she poured them a cup of hot coffee and smiled. A small boy of about three years peeked around the corner of her skirts and ran into his father's arms. Simon Maxwell, farmer, lawyer and pioneer, picked up his son and threw him into the air, gave him a kiss on the cheek, then gently sat him in his grandfather's lap to be cuddled and admired.

Ezekiel remained in the city until his death in 1871 and was buried in the local church cemetery under the tall trees. He seemed content in the final years of his life, as he watched the young family grow and mature. He loved all his children and grandchildren but in the parlor of his daughter's home, he found a peace that eluded him in the Boston of his earlier years. By that time, Susannah had four children, three boys and one girl, and Simon Maxwell's practice in law had eclipsed anything he'd expected to achieve.